Wings and Tales

Wings and Tales

Learning About Birds Through Folklore, Facts, and Fun Activities

Jennifer L. Kroll

With Story Illustrations by Teresa A. DelVecchio

A Teacher Ideas Press Book

LIBRARIES UNLIMITED

AN IMPRINT OF ABC-CLIO, LLC
Santa Barbara, California • Denver, Colorado • Oxford, England

Library of Congress Cataloging-in-Publication Data

Kroll, Jennifer L.
  Wings and tales : learning about birds through folklore, facts, and fun activities / Jennifer L. Kroll.
    p. cm.
  Includes index.
  Summary: "Parents and teachers can use this book to engage children with the world outside by opening their eyes to fascinating common bird species" — Provided by publisher.
    ISBN 978-1-59884-597-6 (pbk.) — ISBN 978-1-59884-598-3 (ebook)
  1. Birds—Identification.   2. Birds—Folklore.   3. Tales.   I. Title.
    QL676.K78   2011
    598—dc22   2010051619

ISBN: 978-1-59884-597-6
EISBN: 978-1-59884-598-3

15 14 13 12 11 1 2 3 4 5

This book is also available on the World Wide Web as an eBook.
Visit www.abc-clio.com for details.

Libraries Unlimited
An Imprint of ABC-CLIO, LLC

ABC-CLIO, LLC
130 Cremona Drive, P.O. Box 1911
Santa Barbara, California 93116–1911

This book is printed on acid-free paper ∞

Manufactured in the United States of America

A Note on the Illustrations

Story illustrations for this book were drawn in pen and ink by Teresa A. DelVecchio, who holds the copyright to these works. Coloring pictures on Feathered Facts File pages were drawn in pen and ink by the author. All pages of this book may be reproduced for teaching purposes. However, illustrations from the book may not be reproduced for other purposes without permission.

Dedication
To my parents, both dedicated teachers.

Contents

Chapter 1

Introduction

Let your kids learn the stories of the birds. The world outside their windows will never look the same again!

GETTING KIDS OUT—AND INTO NATURE

"Learning the Birds" has long been a common component of early-grade science curriculum; and today, more than ever, it's an important practice. In the past few years, experts in a number of different fields have come together to point out the pitfalls of today's **overly plugged-in childhoods.** Studies show that on average today's children spend half as much time outdoors as children did 20 years ago (Juster, Omo, and Stafford 8), and many spend as much as six hours a day in front of computer, television, or video game screens (Roberts, Foehr, and Rideout 6). At the same time, the percentage of obese children in the United States has risen sharply. According to the Centers for Disease Control and Prevention, "several studies have found a positive association between the time spent viewing television and increased prevalence of **obesity** in children" (CDC). Similarly compelling evidence links lack of outdoor time with **childhood depression** (Louv 47–49) and with a rise in diagnoses of **hyperactivity disorders** among children (Louv 98–111). Some people also worry that kids with little connection to nature may not grow up to be responsible caretakers of our planet (Louv 3, 133). With all of these concerns in mind, the National Wildlife Federation recently encouraged parents and educators to make sure that children get at least one "Green Hour" of free time outside per day (National Wildlife Federation).

The curriculum in this book is designed to encourage young people—and their teachers and parents—to get outside and become interested in an aspect of nature that is a visible part of most of our everyday lives. Whether children live in an urban center, suburban

1

environment, or rural area, many of the common North American birds presented in this book are sure to be neighbors.

TALES FOR ALL TIMES . . .

Once upon a time, not that long ago, each of these winged neighbors had a story to tell. Legends and folklore about birds abound in almost every culture. This book brings together a sampling of these bird tales, retold in a way that makes them especially relevant and fun for today's children. Each selected tale revolves around a particular familiar North American bird species and introduces attributes of that species in a memorable way. Bird species covered in *Wings and Tales* include the blue jay, cardinal, chickadee, crow, dove, gull, hawk, hummingbird, loon, mallard duck, meadowlark, mockingbird, owl, robin, sparrow, barn swallow, swan, turkey vulture, woodpecker, and wren.

Some of the tales retold in *Wings and Tales* are Native American in origin. Others have their roots in cultures of Europe, Asia, or Africa. Many reflect on universal themes such as generosity, self-acceptance, gratitude, justice, responsibility, leadership, and friendship. The stories in this volume therefore can serve as a springboard not only for discussion of animal characteristics, but also for reflection on human values and behavior. The **Discussion or Writing Prompts** provided in the introduction to each chapter can help parents and teachers get children to connect with the stories on a deeper level and make discoveries about themselves, while also practicing important communication skills.

. . . AND ALL AGES

Most stories in this volume are appropriate for children of a wide range of ages. Young children can enjoy listening as teachers and parents read the stories and facts aloud or use the Story Sharing Strategies to present and perform the material in creative ways. Teachers also can copy the **folktale** and **Feathered Facts File** pages and pass them out to children for group or independent reading. To help parents and teachers make the most appropriate story selections, the reading level of the material in each chapter is indicated on the chapter's introductory page. A general guideline for grade appropriateness of stories and activities is also provided.

MAKING CROSS-CURRICULAR CONNECTIONS

We often tend to teach the various subjects separately from one another. We teach math, then move on to reading, then to writing, and history, science, and so forth. But the world outside of the front door, or the schoolhouse door, is rich with examples of how these areas of learning overlap and intersect in myriad ways. This book was inspired by the belief that children are fully capable of and enjoy making these broader connections, and that many do their best learning when they are prompted to use their various capacities, such as sensing, thinking, and feeling, at once. The hands-on **Extension Activities** provided in each chapter of Wings and Tales allow teachers and parents to segue seamlessly from working with children on **listening, reading, and communication skills,** to helping them develop an understanding of **math and science concepts** such as:

- The food chain
- Measuring
- Estimation
- Adaptation
- Making and interpreting charts
- Animal characteristics and behavior
- Collecting data
- Comparing and contrasting

In addition to the Extension Activities, each chapter of *Wings and Tales* also provides a **Be a Backyard Birder Tip.** These can inspire children to learn about animal characteristics and behavior by observing and interacting with backyard birds in fun, educational, and species-appropriate ways.

USING THIS BOOK WITH ESL/EFL LEARNERS

Folktales such as those in this book may be a good choice of material for ESL and EFL learners. In her article "Story Grammars and Oral Fluency" in the *Journal of the Imagination in Language Learning and Teaching*, Professor Dafne Gonzales suggests the use of stories, and particularly folktales, "to enhance recall" among English language learners, as well as to "increase motivation and promote oral fluency while reinforcing other skills" (Gonzalez 74). Folktales and fairy tales are told all over the world. And while the elements of these tales differ from culture to culture, the basic folktale form is likely to feel familiar to many English language learners. The feeling that "I already know how this kind of story goes" may inspire ESL/EFL readers to press on, making educated guesses, when they encounter unfamiliar words and phrasing in reading material. And the recall and retelling of stories such as folktales is, as Gonzales suggests, an excellent practice strategy. The stories in *Wings and Tales* are especially appropriate for EFL/ESL learners in that the majority of them are written at about a second-grade reading level. Yet, unlike some other easy-reading material intended for young children, these tales can appeal to a broader audience including older children and even adults.

When reading aloud to ESL/EFL learners, it is best to provide some visual cues that can help listeners follow the story. Some of the **Story Sharing Strategies** in this book are suggestions for adding in such visual elements. In general, felt boards and puppets are excellent tools for making storytelling a more visual affair for children. Storytellers and audience members can also use props, don costumes, or act out portions of the story. Storytellers or readers can ask questions during and after the story to assess comprehension. English language learners can be prompted to practice language skills by retelling the stories they've read or heard. All of the hands-on extension activities presented in *Wings and Tales* also can be used, or adapted for use, with ESL/EFL students.

USING BOOK CHAPTERS IN THE CLASSROOM OR HOME SCHOOL SETTING

Each chapter of this book focuses on a particular bird species. Chapters break down into four sections as follows:

1. Parents and Teacher Page

The introduction section contains background information for parents and teachers, as well as ideas for presenting the material to children and prompting children to discuss and write about what they've heard or read.

2. Folktale

The second portion of each chapter is a folktale (or other similar tale) that revolves around a bird character or characters of the featured species. These tales can be used with other chapter material or read on their own. You may choose to copy the tales and give a copy to each child present. Children in grades two and up, and some younger, may be able to read these tales independently, or to follow along while you read aloud. These fictional tales all emphasize some real-life aspect of the bird species depicted. For instance, the tale "The Princess and the Jaybird" offers an explanation for how jays came to have blue feathers and harsh-sounding voices. With young children, it may be beneficial to have an after-reading discussion about what is real and what is not real in each story. Illustrations accompany the stories. However, you may choose to have children listen to the story and then create their own illustrations based on what they imagine.

3. Feathered Facts File

The third item in each chapter is the **Feathered Facts File.** This provides scientific information about the bird species presented in simple language. These pages may be photocopied and passed out to children for independent reading or so that children can follow along while you read. Each **Feathered Facts File** page contains a picture of the bird species that is suitable for children to color. Coloring in these images may help children retain what they've learned about bird coloration and other aspects of appearance. You may wish to present children with a full-color photograph of the species so that they can use this as a model while they color their pictures. Or you can prompt children to develop their research and computer literacy skills by searching out photographs of the birds in a library, field guide, or online source. Multiple photographs of each bird species in this book can be found on Cornell University's All About Birds Web site (www.allaboutbirds.com).

4. Extension Activity

The final portion of each chapter features a hands-on Extension Activity. Some of these activities tie in closely with the chapter's folktale, as is the case with the "Solving the Pitcher Problem" activity in Chapter 5 or the "Big Bird, Little Bird" activity in Chapter 21. Other extension activities, however, can be undertaken without reading the folktale presented in the chapter. A few activities, such as "Feather Functions" (Chapter 12) or "Recycle Bin Birdfeeders" (Chapter 4), may be fitted quite easily into the study of other bird species beyond the particular species represented in the chapter. Each Extension Activity begins with a list of items needed to perform or carry out the activity. Step-by-step instructions follow for parents and teachers who will be leading these activities.

USING THIS BOOK TO MEET NATIONAL LANGUAGE ARTS STANDARDS

You can use this book's folktales, nonfiction selections, story sharing suggestions, and writing and discussion prompts to help your students meet the language arts standards set jointly by the National Council of Teachers of English (NCTE) and the International Reading Association (IRA). A number of the Extension Activities in *Wings and Tales* also can be used to help children develop communication and research skills referenced in the NCTE/IRA standards. On NCTE's Web site, the organization reminds teaching professionals that "these standards are interrelated and should be considered as a whole, not as distinct and separate" (NCTE). The standards are as follows.

NCTE/IRA Standards for the English Language Arts

1. Students read a wide range of print and nonprint texts to build an understanding of texts, of themselves, and of the cultures of the United States and the world; to acquire new information; to respond to the needs and demands of society and the workplace; and for personal fulfillment. Among these texts are fiction and nonfiction, classic and contemporary works.

2. Students read a wide range of print and nonprint texts to build an understanding of the many dimensions (e.g., philosophical, ethical, aesthetic) of human experience.

3. Students apply a wide range of strategies to comprehend, interpret, evaluate, and appreciate texts. They draw on their prior experience, their interactions with other readers and writers, their knowledge of word meaning and of other texts, their word identification strategies, and their understanding of textual features (e.g., sound-letter correspondence, sentence structure, context, graphics).

4. Students adjust their use of spoken, written, and visual language (e.g., conventions, style, vocabulary) to communicate effectively with a variety of audiences and for different purposes.

5. Students employ a wide range of strategies as they write and use different writing process elements appropriately to communicate with different audiences for a variety of purposes.

6. Students apply knowledge of language structure, language conventions (e.g., spelling and punctuation), media techniques, figurative language, and genre to create, critique, and discuss print and nonprint texts.

7. Students conduct research on issues and interests by generating ideas and questions, and by posing problems. They gather, evaluate, and synthesize data from a variety of sources (e.g., print and nonprint texts, artifacts, people) to communicate their discoveries in ways that suit their purpose and audience.

8. Students use a variety of technological and information resources (e.g., libraries, databases, computer networks, video) to gather and synthesize information and to create and communicate knowledge.

9. Students develop an understanding of and respect for diversity in language use, patterns, and dialects across cultures, ethnic groups, geographic regions, and social roles.

10. Students whose first language is not English make use of their first language to develop competency in the English language arts and to develop understanding of content across the curriculum.

11. Students participate as knowledgeable, reflective, creative, and critical members of a variety of literacy communities.

12. Students use spoken, written, and visual language to accomplish their own purposes (e.g., for learning, enjoyment, persuasion, and the exchange of information).

(*Standards for the English Language Arts*, by the International Reading Association and the National Council of Teachers of English, Copyright 1996 by the International Reading Association and the National Council of Teachers of English. Reprinted with permission.)

USING THIS BOOK TO MEET NATIONAL SCIENCE STANDARDS

Teachers also can use the reading material and activities suggested in this book to help students to achieve many of the outcomes detailed in the National Academy of Science's 2008 publication, *National Science Education Standards*. In this publication, the National Academy of Sciences (NAS) states that as a result of classroom activities, students should develop a number of abilities related to scientific investigation, as well as an understanding of important scientific concepts. NAS fits these abilities and concepts into the following eight categories: (1) Unifying Concepts and Processes; (2) Science as Inquiry Standards; (3) Physical Science Standards; (4) Life Science Standards; (5) Earth and Space Science Standards; (6) Science and Technology Standards; (7) Science In Personal and Social Perspectives Standards; (8) History and Nature of Science Standards (NAS 103–111).

Through reading the **Feathered Facts File** pages and learning about the bird species covered in *Wings and Tales*, K-4 level students can achieve all three of the educational outcomes that NAS lists under the heading "Life Science Standards" (109). Namely, the students will develop an understanding of (1) the characteristics of organisms, (2) the life cycle of organisms, and (3) organisms and environments.

Almost all of the **Extension Activities** suggested in *Wings and Tales* will further aid in the achievement of the outcomes listed under NAS's Life Science Standards. A number of these **Extension Activities** will also help children achieve outcomes associated with other NAS standards for grades K-4 and 5–8, including the Science as Inquiry Standards, the Physical Science Standards, the Science and Technology Standards, and the Science in Personal and Social Perspectives Standards. For example, the Recycle Bin Birdfeeders activity suggested in *Wings and Tales* on page 31, can help children develop "abilities of technological design," one of the desired outcomes detailed under the Science and Technology Standards for both levels K-4 and 5–8 (107).

"The Extension Activities: Skills and Concepts" chart that follows shows how specific activities from *Wings and Tales* relate to the various NAS categories of science standards. It also lists language arts and math skills that can be developed through the completion of the extension activities.

EXTENSION ACTIVITIES: SKILLS AND CONCEPTS

		Bird Food Muffins (p. 15)	Need for Seeds (p. 23)	Recycle Bin Birdfeeders (p. 31)	Pitcher Problem (p. 38)	Flock Walk (p. 45)	Into the Wind (p. 54)	Hawk Eyes Walk (p. 64)	Hummingbird Garden (p. 70)	Adapted for Diving (p. 78)	Duck Duck Games (p. 86)	Feather Functions (p. 92)	Song Recorders (p. 99)	Food Chain Flip Game (p. 107)	Worm Watch (p. 114)	Pinecone Birdfeeder (p. 122)	Two Views (p. 131)	Rescue Role Play (p. 138)	Vulture Venn (p. 144)	Code Woodpecker (p. 152)	Big Bird, Little Bird (p. 158)
Science As Inquiry Standards	observing nature				x		x						x		x		x			x	
	collecting and analyzing data												x		x		x	x			
	conducting experiments				x					x											
	using tools: pedometer							x													
	using tools: compass					x															
	using tools: magnifiers																x				
Physical Science Standards	properties of objects				x																
	motions/forces				x																
Life Science Standards	understanding characteristics of animals	x		x		x	x	x	x	x	x	x	x	x	x		x	x	x	x	x
	understanding characteristics of plants								x							x					
	adaptations									x									x		
	the food chain													x					x		
Science and Technology Standards	making and testing design choices				x																
Science In Personal and Social Perspectives Standards	recycling			x																	
	impact of human behavior on animals/habitats									x									x		
Math Skills	measuring	x	x																		x
	estimation		x																		
	sorting objects								x			x									
	using a Venn diagram																		x		
	using fractions																				x
	making a graph, chart, or map							x			x										
Language Arts Skills	spelling and reading													x							
	listening skills												x							x	
	comparing and contrasting																x		x		x
	presenting ideas orally																	x			
	using research skills																		x		
	coding and decoding																			x	

Chapter 2

Blue Jay

Appropriate for grades:

K-4

Reading level of story and fact file:

2.1

INTRODUCTION FOR PARENTS AND TEACHERS

Jays are common neighborhood birds with very distinctive coloring. Because of this, they may be among the first birds that children learn to identify. Blue jays are common throughout much of the United States and Canada. They are extending their range and are even seen regularly in some places on the Pacific Coast. However, children living in western states and provinces may be more familiar with other related jays such as Steller's jays and western scrub-jays.

Jays are native not only to North America. Forty species can be found throughout the world. The folktale in this chapter comes from India. It is pourquoi story that explains how the jay not only got its lovely blue coloring, but its harsh, squawky voice. For alternative versions of the story, see the Works Consulted list on p. 161.

Much of the information about blue jays in this chapter, including that presented in the **Feathered Facts File,** is taken from Cornell University's *All About Birds* Web site. You can visit this site at http://www.allaboutbirds.org/guide/Blue_Jay/lifehistory to learn more, find photographs of blue jays, and to play recordings of their calls.

Along with the story and facts in this chapter, you may also wish to introduce children to Anne Rockwell's lovely picture book, *Two Blue Jays* (New York: Walker & Company,

9

2003). It tells the story of school children watching blue jays nesting outside their classroom window.

STORY SHARING STRATEGY

Have children help you perform "The Princess and the Jaybird" using a puppet theater and stuffed birds or bird puppets. You will need two birds, one that is brown and one that is blue (preferably a blue jay). You will also need a blue scarf. Designate a princess from among the children present. The princess can wear a tiara or other crown to indicate her status. The princess can wrap the brown bird in the blue scarf. Then, behind the scenes, the blue bird can be exchanged for the brown beneath the scarf.

DISCUSSION OR WRITING PROMPT

The princess in this story spends a lot of time feeling down about the one thing in her life that isn't perfect. This keeps her from enjoying all the other good things in her life. Do you ever act like this? Do you spend too much time thinking or worrying about the one bad thing you wish you could change? What is your one bad thing?

The Princess and the Jaybird

A folktale from India as told by Jennifer Kroll

In the olden days, in India, there lived a princess. The princess was lucky, for she had all the good things in life. She was pretty and elegant. She wore fine clothes and lived in a lovely palace. Beside the palace was a garden full of birds and flowers. There she could sit and dream away her days.

You would think that such a lucky girl would also be happy. But this princess was not; for though her life was nearly perfect, the princess had one problem. That problem was her voice. The princess had a voice that just wasn't princessy. It was deep and scratchy. Her voice was always just a little bit too loud. It was bossy sounding, too. The princess knew that people found her voice annoying. And she tried to change it—she really did. She tried to speak in a pleasant, soft way. But her words always came out bossy and harsh and much too loud—not princessy at all.

Many young men admired the princess, in spite of her voice. She was very pretty, after all. But the princess did not care for any of these young men. She only had eyes for handsome Prince Rama. And Prince Rama never paid her any attention. He had no idea how pretty she was. Prince Rama, you see, was blind.

"If only I could change my voice," the princess sighed as she sat in her garden. "Then Prince Rama might love me." It was a beautiful spring day. Birds were singing all around her. Flowers were blooming. But the princess was not enjoying any of this. The princess was too busy feeling sorry for herself.

Of all the birds in the garden, the jay had the most beautiful voice. The princess listened for a moment to the song pouring from this plain brown bird. "How beautiful your voice is, Jaybird," she sighed. "If I had your voice, then Prince Rama would surely love me. Jaybird, Jaybird, give me your voice!" she cried out. And tears trickled down her cheeks.

"Don't cry, Princess," said a voice.

The princess looked up in surprise. She saw that the jaybird had hopped down to a nearby branch. It was looking at her with concern.

"Jaybird?" the princess said. "Did you speak to me just now?"

"I did," said the jaybird in its lovely voice. "I wish you would stop crying. For I am happy to grant your wish. I will give you my voice."

"But how can you do that?" asked the stunned princess. "How can you give me your voice?"

"There is a pond not far from here," said the jay. "I can tell you the way. Inside the pond grows a magic lotus flower. Wait until night. Go to the pond and pick a lotus flower. And then speak your wish. It will be granted."

The princess could hardly believe what the bird told her. She did not know what to think. Yet, that night, when everyone else was in bed, she got up. The night was chilly. So the princess threw her beautiful blue silk scarf around her shoulders. She quietly tiptoed from the palace.

The princess walked through the woods until she came to the pond. In the waters of the pond grew a single lotus flower. Filled with hope, the princess plucked the flower. She held the flower against her heart. Then she spoke her wish.

"I wish," she said, "that I could have the lovely voice of the jaybird. I wish I could have it instead of my own voice."

At that moment, the moon seemed to glow a little brighter. The princess felt a tingling feeling in her head, her heart, and her throat. The magic seemed to be working! She opened her mouth to speak, and a new voice came pouring out. It was soft. It was sweet. It was musical. It was just like the voice of the jaybird.

"Hurrah! My voice is changed!" she sang out. "Thank you, Jaybird!"

"You're welcome," came a loud, harsh voice nearby.

The princess looked up. And there was the jaybird, perched on a nearby tree.

"Jaybird—your voice, your beautiful voice!" the princess cried. "You sound— you sound like me!"

"Yes," croaked the jaybird. "I've got your voice. And you've got mine. I hope now you can be happy."

But the princess suddenly felt bad about what she'd done. "I should not have asked you for your voice," she realized. "I already had so many things. I had beautiful clothes and a lovely home. My family loved me. And everyone told me how pretty I was. All you had was your beautiful voice. I should not have taken it from you."

"I wanted to give my voice to you," croaked the bird.

"But now you have nothing!" cried the princess. "You are just a plain, brown bird. Your voice was the one thing that made you special."

     The Princess and the Jaybird

"Ah, but you are wrong," said the jaybird to the princess. "My voice wasn't the thing that made me special. I still am special. It isn't how you look or sound or what you have that makes you special. You're special because of how you are on the inside. Didn't you know that, Princess?"

"I didn't," said the princess, feeling ever more ashamed. "Thank you for your wisdom, Jaybird. And thank you for your beautiful voice. I only wish I had a gift to give you in return." And she looked about her for anything she could give the bird. All she had with her was her blue silk scarf. "Here," she said, taking the scarf from her shoulders. "It is chilly tonight. Take my scarf. It is not much of a gift, but it will keep you warm." And she wrapped the beautiful blue silk scarf around the bird. "I wish," the princess said, "that you could have feathers this color and wear them always. For that would be a much better gift."

As she said it, the moon got a little brighter. And suddenly the princess found herself staring at a bird covered in beautiful blue feathers.

"But how . . .?" she cried.

"It is the magic lotus," said the jaybird in its new harsh voice. "You're still holding it. It has granted you a second wish."

And so it had.

And from that day to this, the jay has had its harsh voice and its beautiful feathers.

And as for the princess, people say that Prince Rama finally noticed her. He fell in love with her and they got married. But with or without her prince, you can be sure of one thing. The princess was a little bit wiser. And so she lived happily ever after.

BLUE JAYS

- Most people think blue jays are pretty birds. With their bright feathers, they are also pretty hard to miss! Blue jays can be seen year-round in parts of the United States east of the Rocky Mountains.

- Acorns are the favorite food of these birds. But blue jays eat other foods, too. Along with nuts and seeds, they eat insects. Once in a while, they also eat other small animals or eggs. They hold food with their feet as they eat.

- A blue jay can carry off five acorns at a time. Jays have a special storage spot in their throats. It's called a *gular pouch*. A blue jay can carry two or three acorns in this pouch. It can hold a fourth acorn in its mouth. Then it snaps up a fifth with the tip of its beak.

- Jays are not known for their pretty singing. Their loud, harsh voices can be heard from far away. Scientists think these birds can say a lot of things to each other.

- Blue jays are good mimics. They can meow like a cat. They sometimes make hawk sounds. They might do that to warn other birds that a hawk is nearby. But sometimes they also do it to scare other birds away from a feeder.

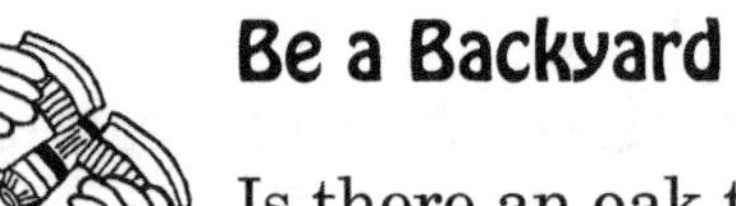

Be a Backyard Birder

Is there an oak tree in your yard or a nearby park? That's a perfect place to watch for blue jays. These birds love to eat the acorns that drop from oaks.

EXTENSION ACTIVITY:
BIRD FOOD MUFFINS (OR ORNAMENTS)

Concepts: animal diets; measuring

For this activity, you will need:

suet

some of the following fillings: crushed peanuts, cracked corn, birdseed, rolled oats, raisins, sunflower seeds

measuring cups

plastic drinking straw(s)

scissors

string, twine, or ribbon

stovetop

refrigerator

stirring spoon

- Many wild birds like to eat suet. It is a concentrated source of calories and can be especially helpful during the winter months, when birds burn many calories trying to stay warm. You can buy suet cakes in many stores.
- Melt suet in a pan over low to medium heat. Older children may be able to do this with some supervision.
- Have children use measuring cups to add fillings, such as crushed peanuts, cracked corn, rolled oats, and raisins to the mix. Appropriate amounts of these secondary ingredients will vary, depending on how much suet you have. If you wish, take the opportunity to point out and discuss the fraction amounts printed on the cups. Give children the opportunity to experiment with filling the cups and to note that, for example, two half cups are equal to one cup.
- Carefully pour the liquid suet and fillings mixture into muffin tins or molds.
- Have children snip straws in halves or thirds.
- Have children place a straw through the center of each muffin, so that the straws are standing straight in the suet mixture. The straw pieces should be pressed in so that each is touching the bottom of the mold or tin.
- Have children refrigerate the muffins for an hour or until the suet is hardened.
- Have children remove the muffins carefully from the tin. You may need to cut around the edge of the muffins with a butter knife.
- Have children remove the straws from each muffin, revealing a hole in the center of the muffin.
- Have children tie a length of string, twine or ribbon onto each suet muffin, threading the line through the center hole.
- Hang the muffins outdoors. These muffins can make nice ornaments for an outdoor Christmas tree. For additional tree decorations, have children string cranberries and peanuts to make an edible garland the birds will love.

Chapter 3
Cardinal

Appropriate for grades:

K-4

Reading level of story and fact file:

2.6

INTRODUCTION FOR PARENTS AND TEACHERS

Northern cardinals are common birds throughout much of the United States and Mexico. Their beautiful colors and sweet song make them a favorite of both children and adult backyard birders. Many children who live with cardinals nearby may already be able identify a male. Children may need assistance in learning to identify females of the species, which have much more muted coloring.

This chapter's story, "How Cardinal Got His Red Feathers," is a Cherokee pourquoi tale. Many different versions of this same story exist. In almost all of them, the red feathers are a reward for an act of kindness. Some of the stories end with the male cardinal's receipt of his red feathers. Others go on to explain why the female cardinal has some red coloration, but less than her mate. For alternative versions of the story, see the Works Consulted list on p. 161.

Much of the information about cardinals in this chapter, including that presented in the **Feathered Facts File,** is taken from Cornell University's *All About Birds* Web site. You can visit this site at http://www.allaboutbirds.org/guide/Northern_Cardinal/id. To find out more about cardinals, see photographs of both males and females, and play recordings of cardinals' songs and calls.

STORY SHARING STRATEGY

Copy and enlarge the image of the cardinal on the Feathered Facts File page. Copy it onto two pieces of brown paper. Ready a dish or cup of red paint and a paintbrush. Use the cut-out birds in your storytelling. When you reach the point in the story where the male cardinal paints himself red, tack the paper bird to an easel or bulletin board. Paint your brown paper cardinal red, or allow the children to do so. Repeat this process to create an appropriately painted female cardinal with red accents on her crest, wings, and tail.

Alternatively, make two copies of the cardinal for each child present. Use plain or light brown paper. Pass the two birds out to each child. Supply the children with red crayons, markers, or paint. Read the story and at the appropriate points in the tale, have the children color Mr. Cardinal and Mrs. Cardinal.

DISCUSSION OR WRITING PROMPT

Say: This story is about a bird who chooses to change the color of his feathers. If you were a bird and could choose feathers of any color, what color feathers would you choose?

To extend the activity, have children describe their birds in writing and draw and color pictures to go with their descriptions.

How Cardinal Got His Red Feathers

A folktale of the Eastern Cherokee as told by Jennifer Kroll

Raccoon is a bit of a smart aleck; and he has always been, since the beginning of time. He likes to tease the other forest animals and play pranks on them. One day, long ago, Raccoon was giving Wolf a hard time. All of a sudden, Wolf got angry.

"I've heard just about enough out of you!" he snarled. He ran at Raccoon with his sharp teeth flashing.

"Uh oh!" said Raccoon. And he bolted up a tree near the riverbank.

Wolves, of course, can't climb trees. All Wolf could do was jump up and lean on the tree trunk with his front paws. "I'm going to get you!" he growled up at Raccoon.

"Well, come on up and get me then," said Raccoon, quite calmly.

But, of course, Wolf could not come up.

"You have to come down sometime," Wolf growled up at Raccoon. "And I'm going to be right here when you do. I'm going to get you. You'd better believe it."

"I'll believe it when I see it," laughed Raccoon.

Wolf paced at the bottom of the tree. An hour went by. But Raccoon didn't come down. After a while, Wolf got tired of pacing. He lay down and put his head on his paws. He gazed up at the branch where Raccoon was sitting.

"You have to come down sometime," Wolf growled again.

"Yes, I suppose I do. Sometime," said Raccoon.

But he did not come down. Another hour or two went by. Finally, Wolf fell asleep at the foot of that tree. And when he was snoring good and loud, Raccoon came down. He was tiptoeing past Wolf when he got the idea for another prank. Raccoon scooped up some mud from the riverbank. He clumped the mud over Wolf's eyes. He packed it on good and heavy. Then, snickering, Raccoon strolled off through the forest.

Wolf stayed asleep a long time. By the time he woke up, the mud had dried hard. It had dried so hard he could not open his eyes. What a panic Wolf was in! He howled and moaned pitifully. He batted at his face with his paws. He stumbled around, bumping into things. Wolf made such a racket that the plain brown bird flying overhead swooped down to see what was the matter.

"What's wrong?" the brown bird asked. "What has happened to you, brother?"

"My eyes! My eyes!" cried Wolf. "I can't see! That nasty Raccoon has played another trick on me."

The brown bird's name was Cardinal. He felt sorry for Wolf. "I can help you," Cardinal said. "Sit still. I'll get the mud off of your eyes."

So Wolf sat still and Cardinal began to peck at the mud. It took a long time for Cardinal to get it all off. But finally Wolf could see again.

"Thank you, kind bird," said Wolf. "And now I must do something to repay you for your trouble."

"It was no trouble," said Cardinal. "And I really should get back to my nest. The little ones are probably hungry. And my missus is surely wondering where I am."

"But you must let me do something for you," said Wolf. "And I know just the thing. Wouldn't you like to have lovely red feathers instead of your plain brown ones?"

"Red feathers?" said Cardinal. He was interested. "Could you really give me red feathers?"

"I know where the humans who live in the village get their red paint," said Wolf. "They go to a place where the rocks are red. They scrape the rock and mix bits of it with water to make their paint. You can use the same paint to make your feathers red."

"But how will I scrape the rock and mix the paint?" asked Cardinal.

"You won't need to," said Wolf. "It has rained a good bit lately. All around the red rocks are puddles full of red paint. Let me show you the way. You would look very handsome with red feathers."

     How Cardinal Got His Red Feathers

Truly, Cardinal had always wished his feathers were not so plain. He thought how surprised his missus would be if he returned home dressed in red feathers. So he agreed. He followed Wolf to the red rocks. He found a puddle of red paint and rolled in it until his feathers were almost all red. Then he flew off home to his nest. He found his wife tending their babies.

"My goodness!" she said when she saw her husband. "Where did you get those beautiful red feathers, dear?"

Cardinal told his wife the story. He told about the wolf and the red rocks and the paint. "You should go and paint yourself, too," he said to her. And he described how to get to the red rocks.

So Mrs. Cardinal flew off to the red rocks. And she began to paint herself with the red paint. But she only got a bit of her tail and wings done before she started to worry about her babies. What if something happened to them while she was away? She would never forgive herself. Surely having red feathers was not as important as keeping her babies safe. Mrs. Cardinal quickly put one last splash of paint on the tip of her crest. Then, she flew off back to her nest.

And that is why today female cardinals only have a few splashes of red on their brown feathers. Male cardinals, on the other hand, are painted red all over.

NORTHERN CARDINALS

- Male cardinals are bright red almost all over.
- Female cardinals look different than males. They are brown with bits of red on their heads, wings, and tails. They have bright orange beaks.
- Cardinals often travel in pairs.

- Male and female cardinals both sing. In fact, they like to do duets. They switch off lines. They sing back and forth to each other.
- Cardinals guard their turf. They can be nasty to other cardinals that are in their space. Cardinals have been known to attack mirrors. They do this because they think the bird in the mirror is a stranger.
- A cardinal has a pointy crest of feathers on its head. But it can put these crest feathers down when it feels relaxed.
- Cardinals eat seeds, fruit, and insects.
- The cardinal is a bird with lots of fans! It is the state bird of seven states. (That's the most of any kind of bird.) The states are Illinois, Indiana, Kentucky, North Carolina, Ohio, Virginia, and West Virginia.

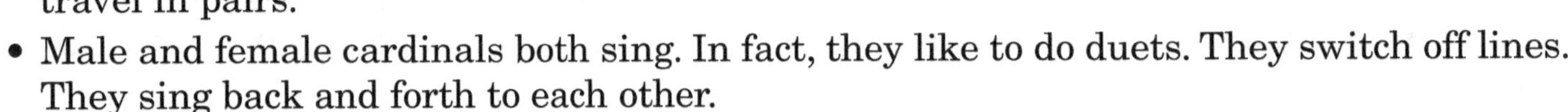

Be a Backyard Birder

Do you want cardinals to come over for lunch? Cardinals prefer a feeder on a post. They don't like a hanging bird-feeder. Put sunflower seeds in your feeder.

EXTENSION ACTIVITY: THE NEED FOR SEEDS: AN ESTIMATION ACTIVITY

Concepts: estimating

For this activity, you will need:

a bag of mixed birdseed or sunflower seeds pencils or markers

a symmetrical birdfeeder paper

a measuring cup newspaper or a drop cloth (optional)

- Prepare materials for the children. Have the feeder, seed, and a cup measure handy. If working indoors, you may wish to put down newspaper or a drop cloth to catch seed spills. If desired, prepare slips of paper on which children can record their estimates.
- Tell children that you want them to estimate how much bird food will be needed to fill the feeder. Explain that an estimate is a good guess. Have children suggest ways to arrive at an estimate.
- Have a child place one level cup of food into the feeder. (To make the math in this activity more challenging for older children, substitute a 2-cup, 1/2-cup, or 1/3-cup measure.)
- Note how full the feeder is after one cup is added. (Mark the level, if you wish.) Then have the children estimate how much food they will need to fully fill the feeder.
- Have children print their names and their estimates on slips of paper. Collect the slips.
- Have the children take turns placing cups of food into the feeder until it is completely full. Have the children count the cups out loud. Or have one child keep a running tally of the cups that have been added.
- Read out the children's estimates to see which children came closest to guessing the actual amount of seeds the feeder holds.

Chapter 4

Chickadee

Content appropriate for grades:

2–6

Reading level of story and fact file:

3.2

INTRODUCTION FOR PARENTS AND TEACHERS

This story differs from others in this collection in that it is the story of a historical figure. Chief Plenty Coups was the last traditional chief of the Crow (or Absalooke, as they call themselves) Indian tribe. The tribal homeland of the Absalooke is in Montana. Plenty Coups is the usual English translation of the Absalooke name Aleek-chea-ahoosh. It means something along the lines of "many achievements" or "many brave deeds." Chief Plenty Coups lived from 1848 to 1932. He fought on the side of the U.S. government during the famous 1876 Battle of the Little Bighorn. He was the only American Indian representative present at the ceremonial dedication of the Tomb of the Unknown Soldier in 1921. His two-story wooden house — as described in the story that follows — still exists. It can be visited at Chief Plenty Coups State Park, which is located near Pryor, Montana.

To learn more about the life of Chief Plenty Coups, you can pick up a copy of *Plenty Coups: Chief of the Crows* by Frank Bird Linderman (University of Nebraska Press, 1962). Linderman was a cowboy poet who used Plenty Coups' own oral recollections to shape his biography. A well-written and visually appealing book about the Crow Indians for children is Edith Tarbescu's *The Crow* (Franklin Watts, 2000). Tarbescu discusses Chief Plenty Coups' life and importance (Tarbescu 38–39), and offers a succinct description of the process of

25

undertaking what the Crow called a *vision quest* in the hopes of seeing one's *medicine animal* (21–22). You can find information about Chief Plenty Coups State Park at Montana's official state Web site: http://fwp.mt.gov/parks/visit/parkSiteDetail.html?id=283264.

A wonderful picture book containing an unrelated Native American chickadee tale is Douglas Wood's *Chickadee's Message* (Adventure Publications, 2009).

Much of the information about chickadees in this chapter, including that presented in the **Feathered Facts File,** is taken from Cornell University's *All About Birds* Web site. You can visit this site at http://www.allaboutbirds.org/guide/Black-capped_Chickadee/id to learn more about chickadees, find photographs of them, and play recordings of their songs.

STORY SHARING STRATEGY

Ask children if anybody had a dream last night. Have children relate recent dreams. Ask whether children found their dreams scary, funny, fun, confusing, or interesting.

Tell the children that this story is about a boy who has a special dream. The dream helps him figure out what kind of person he should be. Explain that people in some countries and cultures think dreams are very important. They believe we can get important messages from our dreams. Explain that the boy in this story was a real person.

DISCUSSION OR WRITING PROMPT

After reading the story, ask children to respond orally or in writing to the following questions. What animal would you have for your medicine animal? What are the strengths of the animal? What is it good at? How might those skills and strengths be useful in your life?

You may also wish to have children draw pictures of their medicine animals.

Dream of a Chickadee:
The True Story of Chief Plenty Coups

As told by Jennifer Kroll

Plenty Coups was a Crow Indian. His people lived—and still live—in what is now the state of Montana. But when Plenty Coups was a boy, Montana was not yet a state. It was a wild land where herds of buffalo roamed. The Crow Indians hunted those buffalo for their meat and skins. They hunted with bows and arrows. They lived as they had for hundreds, maybe thousands, of years. But the world of the Crows was about to change. Soon, white people would settle this area. Local Indians would fight battles against U.S. soldiers. Many tribes would lose much of their land.

The Crows believe that some dreams are very important. These special dreams don't happen often. They teach the dreamer things that he or she needs to know. Crow Indians also believe that one kind of animal is special to each person. A person's special animal is called his or her "medicine." The medicine animal might be a wolf or a bear or a buffalo. It could be any kind of animal. A person shares the strength of his or her special animal. Some people learn about their medicine animal from a dream.

Plenty Coups was just a boy when he had a special dream. The dream changed his life. It also taught him about his medicine animal. In the dream, a guide came to Plenty Coups. The guide led Plenty Coups up onto a hill. "Look there," said the guide in the dream. And Plenty Coups looked. He dreamed he saw buffalo coming out of a hole in the earth. Herds and herds of buffalo came up out of the hole. Soon the plains were thick with buffalos. And then the buffalos stopped coming. The buffalos on the plains all wandered away. Pretty soon, Plenty Coups couldn't see a single buffalo anywhere. "What has happened to all the buffalos?" Plenty Coups wondered.

Then: "Look!" his dream guide said again. And Plenty Coups dreamed he saw more animals come out of the ground. But these were a new kind of animal. Thousands of these new animals came out. They stood grazing where the buffalos had stood. The animals had spotted bodies. Their tails were longer than buffalo tails. The animals looked very strange to Plenty Coups.

Then the dream guide said, "Come." And the guide led the dreaming boy to another place. Plenty Coups saw an old man sitting under a tree in front of a house. The old man was alone. The house was square and made of wood. It had two stories. Plenty Coups' people did not live in wood houses. He had never seen a house like this before. "Who is this old man?" Plenty Coups wondered. "You see yourself," the dream guide told him. "This is how you will be one day."

After that, the dream guide led the dreamer to one last place. The guide showed Plenty Coups a forest of many trees. In the dream, a giant storm came. Winds whipped from all directions. All the trees in the forest began to fall. When the wind let up, only one tree was left standing. "Look," said the dream guide. Plenty Coups looked. "That tree is the home of the chickadee," said the guide. And on a branch of the tree Plenty Coups saw a chickadee.

When Plenty Coups woke up, he remembered his dream. He remembered the strange animals and the square house and the trees falling. He remembered seeing the old man. But he did not know what any of these things meant.

There was one thing he did know, though. He knew his medicine animal was to be the chickadee. The chickadee is just a small bird. It is not a large, fierce animal. But chickadees are smart. They watch and learn. They also can survive tough times. Other animals hibernate or fly south when the weather gets cold, but chickadees stay put. They tough out even the coldest winters. Plenty Coups knew that in his life he would need to be like a chickadee.

Plenty Coups wanted to find out more about his dream. He told the dream to older, wiser members of his tribe. These elders told him what the dream meant. They told him that he had seen the future.

"You saw the buffalo go away," said an elder. "That is going to happen. The white people's cows will graze where buffalo do now."

"You saw yourself alone as an old man," explained an elder. "That means you will have no children."

"You saw a terrible storm," an elder told him. "That means we are in for hard times. All the trees that fell down in your dream are tribes of people. Some of these tribes are our neighbors. They will be badly hurt, perhaps destroyed, in the days to come."

"But in my dream, one tree survived," said Plenty Coups. "It was the tree with the chickadee in it."

"That is the tree of our people," an elder explained. "Your dream is telling you that our people can survive. But we will need to be like the chickadee. We will need to use our brains. We will need to watch and learn."

As Plenty Coups grew up, he won respect for his many brave deeds. But he knew brave deeds alone would not save his people. His people would need to act wisely. They would need to watch and learn. Plenty Coups became the chief of his tribe at a tough time. U.S. troops were fighting with Indian tribes. But Plenty Coups believed his people could not win in a war against the whites. He did not try to fight. Instead, he learned about the white peoples' laws. He went to Washington, D.C., and met with leaders to make deals. The U.S. government did not always keep their deals with Plenty Coups. But Chief Plenty Coups did keep his people on part of their homeland.

Plenty Coups lived to be an old man. He saw white settlers move in and Montana become a state. He lived to see the buffalo disappear and cows graze where they had been. And at the end of his life, he lived in the two-story house he had seen in his dream. He had no children who lived to be adults. "All the Crow Indians are my children," he would say.

Plenty Coups always remembered his special dream. He remembered how the tree of the chickadee had been the one left standing. He told his people to be like the little bird that watches and learns. He told them to get as much education as they could. He made sure Crow children went to school. "Education is your greatest weapon," Chief Plenty Coups said. "With education you are the white man's equal. Without education you are his victim and so shall remain all of your lives."

BLACK-CAPPED CHICKADEES

- Black-capped chickadees don't actually wear caps, of course! The tops of their heads are colored black. These little birds also look like they are wearing black bibs. They have dull orange patches on each side of their bodies.

- Chickadees call chick-a-dee-dee-dee to warn other birds of danger. More dees at the end mean greater danger. Chickadees know to get to safety when they hear this call. And so do some other kinds of birds!

- Chickadees make other sounds, too. They put sounds together in many ways. Scientists have studied chickadee sounds. They think the sounds work much like a language.

- Black-capped chickadees sleep and nest in little cubbyholes. The holes can be in trees, shrubs, or the sides of buildings.

- Black-capped chickadees eat mostly bugs in the summer. They eat bugs, seeds, and berries in the winter. They hide seeds so that they can eat them later. Each seed is hidden in a different spot. A chickadee can keep track of seeds that are in thousands of different spots.

Be a Backyard Birder

Chickadees like to visit bird feeders in the winter. To invite them over for lunch, put out sunflower seeds or peanuts. Don't expect them to hang around while they eat, though. Chickadees tend to just grab a seed and go.

EXTENSION ACTIVITY:
RECYCLE BIN: BIRD FEEDERS AND HOUSES

Concepts: animal behavior; recycling; making design choices and testing out those choices

For this activity, you will need:

one or more containers such as a plastic
  milk jug, quart-sized juice carton, or
  plastic coffee container

scissors

ruler

pencil

paint (optional)

sandpaper (optional)

glue (optional)

craft sticks or twigs (optional)

stickers (optional)

string, thin rope, or chain

- Talk with children about how important it is to reuse and recycle. Prompt children to tell you different items that can be reused or recycled.

- Bring out a bin full of empty containers (orange juice, milk, coffee, etc.). Tell children that they are going to reuse these old containers, making them into bird feeders (or houses). Prompt children to select the containers they wish to work with. If desired, show children an example of a feeder (or house) that has been made from a similar container.

- Talk about what elements a bird feeder (or bird house) needs. Have children help you make a list on a piece of paper or on the board. For instance, for a feeder the list might include: an opening so that birds can get at the food, an opening for filling the feeder, a string or cord for hanging the feeder, and so forth.

- Prompt students to think about possible problems that might occur if the feeder (or house) is not designed well. Again, have children help you make a list. For a feeder, problems might include: food falling out, birds not being able to get to the food, food getting soaked when it rains, squirrels dumping out the food, and so forth.

- Have children plan their feeders, drawing their plans on paper and/or drawing on their chosen containers with pencil or markers.

- Have children cut out any desired openings on the containers. You may need to help children by making an initial hole in the surface of each container. You can do so using a knife or sharp scissors blade. You may also need to help children poke holes in the container for the string or chain, as well as drainage holes. (Make sure any drainage holes are not so large that seed can fall out through them.)

- Have children attach the chain, string, or rope for hanging the feeder (or house).

- Prompt children to paint the feeders (houses), if desired. Special paint that adheres to plastic is available at craft shops and hardware stores. For best results, plastic should be sanded down prior to painting.

- Alternatively, prompt children to decorate their feeders (houses) in some other way, as with stickers, or by gluing craft sticks or twigs to the outside of a milk or juice carton.

- Have children hang their feeders (houses) in an appropriate location.

- Give children the opportunity to report back later on their feeders (houses). Have they seen any bird (or squirrel) activity at the feeder (or house)? Has the child discovered a design problem of any kind? If design problems have been detected, you may wish to give children the opportunity to try the project again, using another technique or other materials.

Chapter 5

Crow

Appropriate for grades:

K-6

Reading level of story and fact file:

3.1

INTRODUCTION FOR PARENTS AND TEACHERS

The featured story in this chapter, "The Crow and the Pitcher," is adapted from a Greek tale recorded in 300 B.C. in a story collection called *Assemblies of Aesopic Tales* or, as we call them today, *Aesop's Fables*. According to tradition, Aesop was a freed slave who lived in ancient Greece from about 620 B.C. to 525 B.C. (Pinkney 9). The stories created or collected by Aesop—or perhaps just credited to him—are short tales featuring mostly animal characters. The tales are intended to educate as well as entertain. "The Crow and the Pitcher" teaches the value of good problem-solving skills. In doing so, it wonderfully illustrates the intelligence and problem-solving capabilities of crows, who can and do use simple tools, just like the crow in the story.

The facts in the fact file section of this chapter pertain to the American Crow, a species common throughout almost all of the United States and much of Canada. Much of the information about crows in this chapter is taken from Cornell University's *All About Birds* Web site. You can visit this site at http://www.allaboutbirds.org/guide/American_Crow/id to learn more about crows, find photographs of these birds, and play recordings of their calls.

STORY SHARING STRATEGY

Read the story aloud to the child or children. Pause when you come to the question, "What should the crow do?" Have the child or children suggest answers. Make a list of all responses. Have the child or children decide which strategy would work the best. Then continue reading the remainder of the story.

Alternatively, gather together props and set them out before reading. Put a small amount of water in a thin-necked container and place it in a tray filled with sand and stones. Present the problem portion of the story. When you reach the question, "What should the crow do?" allow the child or children to examine and manipulate the props in an attempt to discover the solution to the problem.

DISCUSSION OR WRITING PROMPT

Tell children: This story comes from a famous, very old story collection called *Aesop's Fables*. Ask: Do you know any other stories from *Aesop's Fables*? Say: The stories in *Aesop's Fables* usually have a moral printed at the end. Ask: What is a moral? If you were going to make up a moral to put at the end of this story, what would it be? Why?

The Crow and the Pitcher

Adapted by Jennifer Kroll from the ancient Greek fable recorded in *Aesop's Fables*

One day, a crow found a pitcher sitting on the rocky ground. She was excited to see that the pitcher had a little water in the bottom of it. It was the driest part of the year and the crow was very thirsty. But the neck of the pitcher was narrow and high and the crow could not get at the water. She pushed and squeezed to get her head down through the opening. But it did not fit. Would she have to go thirsty with water so close? What should the crow do?

The crow thought and thought, trying to find a way to solve her problem. First, she wondered if she could tip over the pitcher and get the water to pour out. So she tried. But the pitcher was just too heavy and she couldn't make it budge.

Next, she looked around for a hollow tube of some kind that she could use as a straw. But nothing close by seemed likely to work. And she didn't want to leave the pitcher. She feared someone else would get the water if she did.

The crow sat on the pitcher's rim and looked down again at the water she could not reach. How frustrated she was! She hopped back down onto the dry ground, covered with stones and a few tough plants. Useless plants and useless stones. But no—not useless!

For suddenly the crow knew that the stones were just what she needed. She picked up a stone and dropped it into the pitcher. Plunk! She heard it hit the water and sink. She picked up another and another, dropping them in, too. As the pitcher filled with stones, the water rose higher and higher. Finally, the water was high enough. The thirsty crow could have her drink.

     The Crow and the Pitcher

CROWS

- Crows are black from their heads to the tips of their tails.
- Crows live in groups. They have close bonds with family members. Crow pairs often stay together for life. Young adult crows sometimes stay near their parents for a few years. They babysit for younger brothers and sisters.

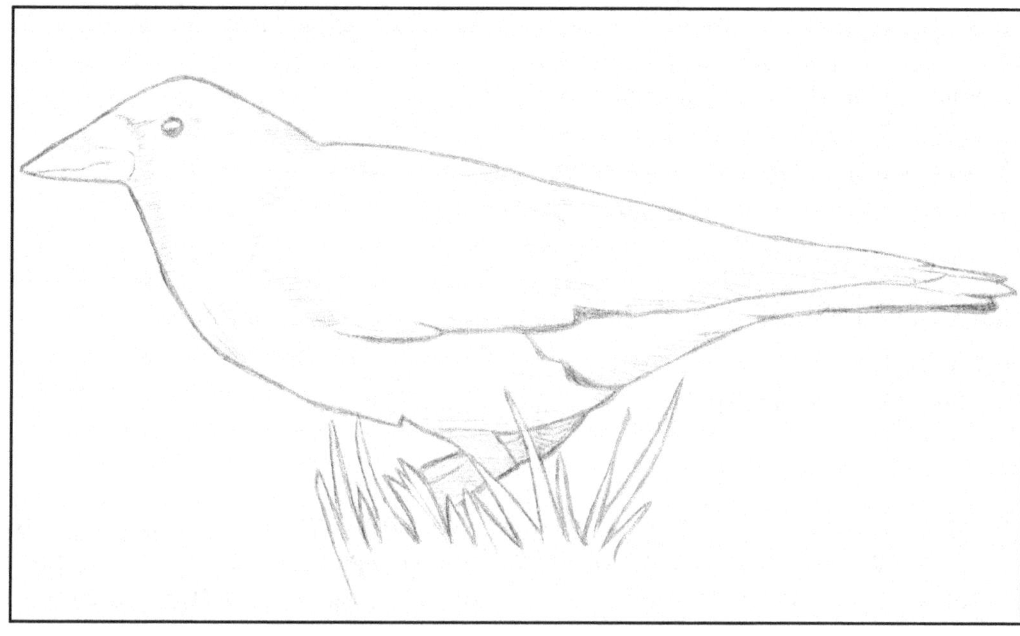

- Crows are very smart and good at solving problems. They can use simple tools. Scientists have filmed crows using sticks to dig grubs out of a tree trunk. Crows in a lab were given narrow jars with food in the bottom. They were also given a straight piece of wire. The crows easily figured out how to bend the wire into a hook. They used the hook to get the food out.
- Crows, like parrots or mockingbirds, can copy sounds. They can copy other birds and animals. They sometimes copy human words and sentences, too.
- Scientists think that crows' voices are all just a little different. Each crow can probably tell who is "talking" when he or she hears another crow.
- Crows can live a pretty long time. One crow kept as a pet lived to be 63!
- Crows eat lots of different things. You might see them eating dead animals along the side of a road (eeuw!). But that's not really their favorite lunch. Crows like to eat seeds, fruit, bugs, grubs, and small animals such as mice and frogs.

Be a Backyard Birder

Crows don't visit bird feeders. But you can still invite these interesting birds to your yard. Leave out some peanuts for them.

EXTENSION ACTIVITY:
SOLVING THE PITCHER PROBLEM

Concepts: displacement and absorption

For this activity, you will need:

a thin-necked pitcher or vase (or two identical pitchers/vases)

water

small stones that will fit into the pitcher/vase

cotton balls, yarn, or strips of cloth

a marker

- After the reading of the story, talk with children about why the crow's solution worked. Ask: "Why did the water rise up when the crow put the stones in the pitcher?" Prompt students to tell you that the water had to move out of the way when the stones were put into the pitcher. The water had no place to go but up.

- Introduce the term *displacement*. Say: "When something moves into a space, forcing something else out, that's called displacement." Explain that every time we move, we are displacing the air around us. Have children move a hand quickly and see if they can feel the air they are displacing.

- Mark the water line on the vase or have a child do so, using the marker.

- Have children take turns (carefully) placing stones in the vase/pitcher until the water is near the top of the vase.

- Mark the water line again with a marker or have a child do so. Mark the top of the stones, also.

- Now empty the stones from the pitcher. Make sure to retain the water, or add water so that the amount is the same as it was before the stones were dropped in.

- Say: "Let's try it again with cotton balls (strips of cloth, etc.)." Have children fill the pitcher/vase with the new substance to the rocks line.

- Have children check to see where the water has reached this time. Is it higher, lower, or the same as last time?

- If the water has not risen as far this time, have the children explain why they think this is the case. Discuss the fact that less water has been displaced because some of the water was absorbed into the cotton balls (strips of cloth, etc.).

Chapter 6
Dove

Appropriate for grades:

K-4

Reading level of story and fact file:

1.7

INTRODUCTION FOR PARENTS AND TEACHERS

The tale in this chapter is adapted from an ancient Indian tale that formed part of a collection of stories called the *Panchatantra.* It is generally believed that the *Panchatantra* was composed in Sanskrit in the second century B.C. However, many of the stories in the cycle were probably already quite old by that time (Ryder 3–4). The tales are similar to *Aesop's Fables* in that each has a strong, clear message or moral—sometimes more than one—about how life works and how to live. According to the traditional introduction to the *Panchatantra*, the stories were written to assist in teaching a king's three foolish and power-hungry sons about the "art of intelligent living" (15). For this reason, the stories reflect on—among other things—the role and proper behavior of a king or leader. This theme is clearly present in "The Doves and the Net." Other strong themes in this story include the importance of friendship and of working together as a team, as well as the danger of just going along with the crowd. All of these themes are certainly as relevant for young people today as they were in the second century B.C. For various versions of "The Doves and the Net" see the Works Consulted list.

Besides containing lessons about human behavior and its consequences, "The Doves and the Net" also reflects some truths about the type of birds depicted. For example, doves

39

do flock in large groups when they are not paired off for mating. They eat seeds and grains off of the ground. And these birds have been and still are commonly hunted for human consumption. In the United States, dove hunting is legal and hunters shoot 20 million mourning doves (the most common type of dove in the United States) each year.

Much of the information about doves in this chapter, including that presented in the **Feathered Facts File,** is taken from Cornell University's *All About Birds* Web site. You can visit this site at http://www.allaboutbirds.org/guide/Mourning_Dove/id to learn more about doves, find photographs of them, and to play recordings of their calls.

STORY SHARING STRATEGY

Before beginning the story, say: "This story is about teamwork." Ask: "What can a team of people do that one person could never do on his or her own?" Have children share their thoughts. Examples might include: playing/winning a soccer game or other sporting event, putting on a play, playing a piece of band or orchestral music, pushing or lifting something heavy, building a large structure such as a bridge, skyscraper, or pyramid, and so forth.

DISCUSSION OR WRITING PROMPT

Have you ever been on a team or worked on anything as part of a team? Describe your experience as a team member. What did you enjoy about being a team member? What did you find difficult?

The Doves and the Net

An Indian tale from the *Panchatantra* as told by Jennifer Kroll

Once upon a time, a group of doves was flying above a forest. As the doves flew over a clearing, several of them looked down.

"Look there!" one dove called. "The ground is covered with grain!"

"There's more than enough for all of us!" said another dove.

"I'm starving. Let's get ourselves some lunch," said a third dove. And they all began diving toward the food.

But the doves were diving into a trap. A hunter had sprinkled the grain on the ground. And as the doves filled their bellies, a net closed upon them all.

"We're trapped!" "I'm stuck!" and "We're done for!" the doves wailed. They flung themselves this way and that. But their fluttering and thrashing did not help at all.

"Listen, my friends!" cried their leader. "You must calm down. You are only wasting your strength. It is true that we are in a big mess just now. We are in great danger. But all of this thrashing will not solve our problem. We got into this mess together. Now we must calm down and work together to get out of it."

"But there is no way out of this net!" cried the panicked doves.

"It's true we can't get out—at least not at the moment," said the leader dove thoughtfully. "But if we work as a team, we can fly away and take the net with us. We can be far from here before the hunter returns."

"Yes!" cried the doves. "Let's do it! Let's get out of here before the hunter comes back!"

"I will give a signal," said the leader dove. "And then we must all fly up at once. We must all fly in the same direction and at the same speed. It will take great teamwork for us to carry away this net. But we are a great team. I know we can do it."

"Teamwork!" the doves all cried. And when their leader gave the signal, they all took off at once.

Up, up they went. And up the net went, too. The doves flew together as if they were one body. And soon they were far away from the place where the hunter had laid the trap for them.

"We've done it!" cried one of the doves. "The hunter will never catch us now."

"But we're still trapped," said another dove. "We must still find a way to get out of this net."

"Listen," said the Leader Dove. "I know a rat who lives just over on the other side of this hill. She is a friend of mine. I have spoken with her often and shared food with her. She is a kind soul and she has very sharp teeth. Perhaps she will help us."

"Let's hope so. It's worth a try," all the doves agreed. And when the leader gave the signal, they landed all together.

From inside one of her tunnels, the rat heard the noise of the flock landing. "Who's there? What's going on?" she called. She fearfully stuck her head out of a hole.

"Rat!" called the leader dove. "It's me, your friend! We doves are in great trouble. We are stuck inside of a hunter's net. But perhaps you can help us. Will you tear a hole in the net with your strong teeth?"

"Of course!" said the rat, stepping out of her hole. "I am always happy to do a favor for a friend."

And the rat began to bite at the ropes of the net. She nibbled and gnawed until she had made a hole large enough for a dove to squeeze through. "I think the hole is big enough now," she said to the leader dove. "Climb through and be free."

But the leader dove would not be the first to leave the net. "It would not be right for me go first," he said. "I must wait until everyone else is safe." He let all the other doves climb out through the hole in the net. When all the others were free, he climbed out at last.

     The Doves and the Net

"Thank you, dear rat," he said to his friend. "You have saved our lives."

"It is my pleasure to help you," said the rat. "I know you would do the same for me."

"Friends," said the leader dove, "are a wonderful thing. With the help of our friends, we can do things we could never do alone."

MOURNING DOVES

- Mourning doves are the most common type of dove in the United States. They live year 'round in most states.
- Mourning doves make a soft coo sound. Some people think these birds sound sad. And that's how they got their name. The word mourning (spelled with a u) means being sad after someone has died.
- Mourning doves are brown and cream, with bits of black. They have long tails and plump bodies.
- Mourning doves eat some berries or a snail from time to time. But mostly they eat seeds, seeds, and more seeds. As they pick seeds off the ground, they store them in a special place inside their throats called a crop. Then they fly up to a safe spot and digest their meal.
- Like many kinds of birds, doves form strong bonds with their mates. Paired doves sit and preen each other's neck feathers. They lock their beaks together and bob their heads up and down. That's pretty lovey-dovey stuff, isn't it? It's no wonder the dove has been a symbol of love for thousands of years in some places.
- Pairs of doves can have up to six broods (or sets) of babies in a year. At first, parents feed their babies a special food called "crop milk." Both mothers and fathers make this food inside their crops. They regurgitate it (throw it up) to feed the babies.

Be a Backyard Birder

Look *under* your bird feeder if you want to see doves. They eat off the ground. You can also find them by using your ears. Listen for their cooing cries. Listen for the whistling sound their strong wings make as they take off.

EXTENSION ACTIVITY: FLOCK WALK

Concepts: animal behavior, flocks and herds, human social behavior

For this activity, you will need:

a variety of play items such as balls, cones, blocks, jump ropes, and so forth

a play parachute with handles

alternatively, strips of cloth large enough to fasten around children's legs or arms and a bag with handles.

- You can complete this activity in your yard, a schoolyard, or any relatively large indoor space. Set out play items such as balls and small cones in varied locations. With larger groups of children, a play parachute will work best for this activity. If you are working with a pair or small group of children, children can be connected leg-to-leg, as they would be for a three-legged race, or with arms bound together.
- Share the tale "The Doves and the Net" with children. Tell children that they are going to pretend to be the doves caught together in the net. They must all move together as a team. Have each child hold a handle of the parachute. Point out the various objects you have placed around the yard or room. Tell children that, working as a team, they must collect all of these objects and place them inside of the parachute. Alternatively, have the children collect the play items into a bag.
- You may wish to time the children and offer some sort of prize for completing the task quickly. You may wish to divide the children into multiple groups and have the groups compete against each other to see which can complete the task most efficiently.
- Once children have finished the activity, ask them questions about the experience: "Was it difficult working together?" "What did you do that made it easier?" and so forth.
- Discuss with children the fact that some types of animals live and move together in groups called flocks or herds. Encourage children to think and talk about the reasons animals do this. What do they gain from being part of the group?

Chapter 7

Gull

Appropriate for grades:

2–6

Reading level of story and fact file:

3.4

INTRODUCTION FOR PARENTS AND TEACHERS

Children seem fascinated by gulls. Small children love to chase these birds. Older children like to watch the antics of these animals as they squabble over food. Children familiar with the Disney movie *Finding Nemo* may recall the humorous scenes in this movie where gulls in a flock compete for food, their calls translated by the animators as: "Mine! Mine! Mine!" Gulls are also sometimes represented in popular culture as symbols of freedom, peace, or achievement. Inspirational posters often feature the image of a gull flying against the back-drop of a sunset.

The tale adapted for presentation in this chapter is an ancient Greek myth that was re-corded in the Roman poet Ovid's *Metamorphoses*. The main characters in the story, the im-prisoned Daedalus and Icarus, view gulls as symbols of freedom. By crafting human-sized wings from sea bird feathers, this father and son escape their prison and manage to soar like the birds. However, the tale ends on a cautionary note. The boy Icarus forgets to follow his father's instructions. Instead of acting with moderation, he soars too high, melting the wax on his wings and crashing into the sea. The tale thus reinforces a Greek philosophical notion famously expressed by the philosopher Aristotle: that "virtue aims at the median" (Aristotle 43) and happiness can be found in sticking to the middle between two extremes.

47

Much of the information about gulls in this chapter, including that presented in the **Feathered Facts File,** is taken from Cornell University's *All About Birds* Web site. You can visit this site at http://www.allaboutbirds.org/guide/Herring_Gull/id to learn more about herring gulls and other gull species, find photographs of them, and play recordings of their calls.

STORY SHARING STRATEGY

Ask children if any of them have ever been inside any kind of a maze. Have children share their experiences. Ask whether the children found their maze experiences fun, exciting, or frightening. Explain that part of the story they are about to read is about a huge maze that has a monster living inside it.

DISCUSSION OR WRITING PROMPT

Ask students: Can you think of something an animal can do that you wish you could do? Have children share responses. Say: "Imagine if you could make a machine or contraption that would let you do what that animal can do. What would it look like?" Have the children draw and color pictures of their animal-inspired inventions. Have them add captions or descriptive text.

Only with Wings:
The Story of Daedalus and Icarus

An ancient Greek myth as told by Jennifer Kroll

Daedalus lived long ago. He lived with his son Icarus on the rocky island of Crete. Daedalus was a man whose mind never stopped working. He was well known for his inventions. He got ideas for many of these inventions from looking at the bodies of animals. For instance, some say he was the first person to put teeth on a saw blade. He came up with the idea while looking at the jawbone of a shark that had washed up on shore.

From the shores of Crete, blue sea stretches out in all directions. The blue sky above Crete is filled with gulls. Today, Crete is a lovely and peaceful place to visit. But legend has it that in Daedalus's day, it was not peaceful. Stories tell of a monster that ran wild on the island of Crete. The monster was called the Minotaur. It looked like a huge man with the head of an angry bull. It killed everything that got in its way. The Minotaur liked nothing better than to eat people for lunch.

The king of Crete at this time was King Minos. And you would think that King Minos would want to get rid of such an awful monster. But legend has it that he did not. King Minos was not a nice guy. He liked having the Minotaur around. The people of Crete were all afraid of the monster. And so King Minos could use the Minotaur to get people to do what he wanted. But he still needed a safe place to keep his monster. A regular cage or pen just would not do. Something better must be built. And so, King Minos called on Daedalus the inventor.

"Daedalus," King Minos said. "I want you to build a pen that will hold my Minotaur. That beast has broken down the walls of every cage I've tried to put him in. But I've heard that you are a great inventor. I know you will think of some way to help me. And for your help, you will be richly rewarded."

Daedalus designed a giant maze, or *labyrinth*, for the king. The maze was very complex and confusing. It had trapdoors and moving walls. The Minotaur would surely never find his way out. King Minos's workers built the maze that Daedalus designed. When it was done, the Minotaur was lured inside.

The labyrinth was a perfect cage for the Minotaur. King Minos was very pleased with Daedalus's work. He gave Daedalus lots of money and a beautiful place to live. It was a very comfortable life for the inventor. Daedalus should perhaps have been happy. But he was not. In fact, he felt terrible about what he had done.

You see, every day, somebody would get thrown into the labyrinth. That person might struggle to find his or her way out. But in the end, the Minotaur would always have his lunch. The roars and screams of the victims could be heard for miles. Every person on the island lived in terror. They all feared they might end up as the Minotaur's next meal. And Daedalus knew that he should not have designed the maze and helped the king.

One day, King Minos's daughter Ariadne came to see Daedalus. She was crying and very upset.

"What's the matter?" asked Daedalus.

"I have fallen in love with Theseus," she bawled. "And tomorrow he is going into the labyrinth. He has volunteered to be the next person thrown inside."

"Why would he do such foolish thing?" asked Daedalus, amazed.

"Theseus says he's going in so that he can kill the Minotaur," Princess Ariadne reported. "He thinks he's going to become a big hero. But I fear he's just going to end up dead like all the others."

"Have you tried to stop him?" Daedalus asked her.

"I can't," wailed Ariadne. "He's determined to go. And my father is happy to let him. Father doesn't like Theseus. Please! I need your help."

Daedalus felt sorry for Ariadne. And so he did a dangerous thing. He told her secrets about the maze. He told her about the places where gates swung shut and the pathways changed. He told her about a way that Theseus could get out of the maze. He drew a map for her to pass along to Theseus.

"That's all the help I can give you," he said. "Theseus will still have to battle the monster and win. That's going be pretty tough. But I sure wish him luck. I wish you both luck."

Ariadne thanked Daedalus and left.

The next day, Theseus amazed everyone. He killed the Minotaur and escaped the maze. After escaping, he went straight to Ariadne. The two of them ran off together. They were far from Crete before King Minos knew what had happened.

King Minos was, of course, angry. And he wasn't just a little bit angry. He was absolutely furious. His monster was dead and his daughter was gone. And, what's worse, she was gone with that troublesome Theseus! How could this have happened? Theseus had somehow known the secrets of the labyrinth. How could he have known? After mulling it over, King Minos had his suspicions. He suspected Daedalus.

Of course, King Minos couldn't really prove that Daedalus had helped Theseus. But even if Daedalus hadn't done so, he still deserved to be punished. That's what King Minos figured. After all, he had told the inventor to design a cage from which nothing could escape. And Daedalus had failed to do this. So King Minos had Daedalus and his son Icarus arrested. The two were dragged to a high stone tower and locked inside. They were given food and kept alive. But they could never go out, except to stand in the wind at the top of the tower. From there, they gazed longingly at the sea. The gulls flying overhead became their friends.

"I wish," sighed Icarus to his father one day, "that we were gulls. For they can come and go as they please. They swoop down if I throw down a few crumbs for them. And then they are off again, while we're stuck here." He tossed down a few crumbs of food and watched the gulls come swooping in.

Daedalus watched the birds, too. "I have been thinking about ways we could break out of this tower," he told his son. "But I'm not sure what we would do next once we got out. I doubt we could make it off of this island in any ship or boat. King Minos's men have been watching the coast very closely. No ship comes or goes without being carefully checked for stowaways. And if we were caught trying to escape, we would surely be killed." Daedalus watched a gull take off into the wind. "It seems to me," he said, "that only with wings can we hope to escape from this island kingdom."

"Alas that we do not have wings like our feathered friends," sighed Icarus. And he picked up a feather left behind by a gull.

"Perhaps we can make some wings," said Daedalus.

And that is what he set out to do.

Daedalus collected feathers from the visiting gulls and other birds. He cemented the feathers together with wax. Daedalus designed two huge sets of wings. The wings were made to work like birds' wings. But they were large enough and strong enough to hold the bodies of humans. Daedalus worked in secret for years on the wings. And then, one day, he and Icarus got their chance to use them and try to escape. Nobody was watching. The wind was strong. Daedalus and Icarus stood atop the tower, wearing their wings.

"We will try to fly across the sea to Greece," Daedalus said to Icarus. "And here is what you must remember on the way. You must not fly too low or too high. If you fly too low, the spray from the waves will wet your wings. They will grow heavy and you will sink. If you fly too high, the heat of the sun will melt the wax that holds your feathers in place. Then your wings will be ruined and down you will fall into the sea. Stick to the middle way. If you stay halfway between the sea and the sky, all will be well."

"I will be careful. I will stick to the middle," promised Icarus. And he and Daedalus jumped from the tower top. Away they flew, like just like birds. And before King Minos could stop them, the two of them were out over the open sea.

Icarus was so happy to be free. After years of living as a captive, he was on his way to a new life. And not only that, but he was flying! This was such fun! Icarus was having such a good time flying that he forgot the promise he had made to his father. Up into the blue sky he soared, closer and closer to the sun. He didn't notice when the wax on his wings began to drip.

"Icarus! Don't fly so high!" Daedalus cried. But his voice got lost in the wind.

Icarus swooped and soared like a gull. And then, suddenly, he was falling. Down, down into the sea he plunged while his father watched in horror. Daedalus could do nothing. He had no way to save his son. He continued on his way to Greece. And there he landed. He was safe, but filled with grief over his lost boy.

Today, the sea between Greece and Crete is called the Icarian Sea. It is named after poor Icarus, who soared too close to the sun and was lost there in the waves.

HERRING GULLS

- Adult herring gulls have white heads and chests and gray backs Young herring gulls look brown and streaked.

- Baby herring gulls touch a red spot on their parents' bills to show they are hungry. Mom and dad gulls both work to feed the babies. They make baby food from food they've eaten. They regurgitate (throw up) the mushed-up food in order to feed their young.

- Herring gulls will eat just about anything. (If you've ever dropped part of your lunch at the beach, you already know that!) They eat fish, other ocean animals, bugs, and eggs. They also eat carrion—which is a fancy word for dead animals.

- Herring gulls have a cool trick for getting clams and oysters out of their shells. The birds grab a closed shell and fly up with it. Then they drop the closed shellfish down onto rocks. Smack! When the shell cracks open, it's snack time!

- Herring gulls like to drink fresh water. But what if the only water around is salty seawater? No problem! The gulls gulp down some seawater. Special glands near their eyes help their bodies filter out the salt. It comes back out of the birds' bills and nostrils.

- In the late 1800s, many herring gulls were killed so that their feathers could be put on hats. In some places, the gulls were wiped out completely. Herring gulls have since made a good comeback.

Be a Backyard Birder

Herring gulls like to rest in open places such as parking lots and airports. Keep an eye out for young birds with brown, streaked, and darker colored bodies.

EXTENSION ACTIVITY: INTO THE WIND

Concepts: using a compass, observing and measuring changes in the environment, observing animal tracks, learning about animal behavior

For this activity, you will need:

a compass

a flag, handkerchief, or kite

- You can complete this activity during a field trip or family trip to a shore where gulls are present. Have the children locate gull footprints in the sand.
- Discuss the footprints. See if the children can figure out which direction the gull was facing when it took off from the ground. (You may have to explain that the gulls' toes face forward.) Explain that all birds take off into the wind. Birds use the wind to help them get up into the air. So by looking at the footprints, children will be able to tell which direction the wind was coming from when the bird took off.
- Have the children use a compass to figure out the direction of the wind at the time when the gull or gulls took off.
- To extend the activity, you might also ask the children: "Is the wind still coming from the same direction as it was when this bird took off?" Have children use a small flag, handkerchief, or even a kite to determine the current direction of the wind and whether there has been a change in wind direction.

Chapter 8

Hawk

Appropriate for grades:

2–6

Reading level of story and fact file:

3.0

INTRODUCTION FOR PARENTS AND TEACHERS

The basic plotline of the Cinderella folktale has traveled far and wide. Versions of this folktale have been recorded in China, Egypt, the Middle East, South America, and just about everywhere else. (See the Works Consulted list for titles of some of these Cinderella versions.) The tale included in this chapter, "The Girl with the Little Gold Star," is a Cinderella story that was told in Spanish-speaking areas of the southwestern United States and in Mexico. The "Fairy Godmother" of Charles Perrault's well-known French Cinderella story is missing from the Little Gold Star story, but she is replaced with other helpful magical figures. In some versions of the story, such as that of Robert D. San Souci, the replacement helper is none other than the Blessed Virgin Mother. However, this chapter's version of "The Girl with the Little Gold Star" borrows the motif of a hawk as a magical helper from Joe Hayes' *Estrellita de oro / Little Gold Star: A Cinderella Cuento* (Cinco Puntos Press, 2000).

   Much of the information about hawks in this chapter, including that presented in the **Feathered Facts File,** is taken from Cornell University's *All About Birds* Web site. You can visit this site at http://www.allaboutbirds.org/guide/Red-tailed_Hawk/id to learn more about red-tailed hawks and other hawks, find photographs of them, and play recordings of their calls.

55

You may also wish to share with children Jeannette Winter's *The Tale of Pale Male: A True Story* (Harcourt, 2007) or Janet Schulman's *Pale Male: Citizen Hawk of New York City* (Knopf, 2008). These picture books tell the story of a hawk pair that famously nested on Fifth Avenue in downtown New York City.

STORY SHARING STRATEGY

When Teresa receives her star in the story, pass out stick-on stars for the listening children to wear on their own foreheads. You may also wish to provide children with scarves to wrap around their heads. The children can cover their own stars with scarves when Teresa's stepmother insists the star be covered. They can uncover their stars at the end of the story when Teresa reveals her star.

DISCUSSION OR WRITING PROMPT

Before or after reading "The Girl with the Little Gold Star," share another version of the Cinderella story such as the Walt Disney movie version, or the classic French fairy tale as recorded by Charles Perrault in 1697 and translated into English by Andrew Lang in 1889. You can find this classic version of Cinderella online at http://www.pitt.edu/~dash/perrault06.html. An award-winning picture book version of Perrault's tale is *Cinderella or The Little Glass Slipper*, translated and illustrated by Marcia Brown (Turtleback, 1997). Prompt children to discuss the similarities and differences between "Cinderella" and "The Girl with the Little Gold Star." Have children help you make a Venn diagram that shows similarities and differences.

The Girl with the Little Gold Star

A Cinderella story from the southwestern United States as retold by Jennifer Kroll

Once there was a girl named Teresa. She lived alone with her father in what is now the state of New Mexico. Teresa's father raised sheep. He spent much time out in the fields with his flock. Teresa liked to help with the sheep, too. She loved animals and had a gentle way with them. But there was always much work for her to do in the house. Teresa's mother had died when she was a baby. And so many household tasks had fallen onto Teresa's shoulders. Teresa mended and weaved and washed and cooked. She did it all cheerfully because she loved her father and knew how much he needed her help.

One day, Teresa's father said to her, "It isn't right that you should always work so hard, Teresa. And it isn't right that you should be alone so much. You have become a lovely young woman. You should be able to enjoy your youth. I want you to have friends your own age to laugh with. I want you to be able to go to parties and dances."

"I'm not unhappy, Father," said Teresa.

"But I want things to be better for you," insisted Teresa's father.

Down the road that led to town lived a widow with two daughters. The daughters were named Laura and Lupe. They were close in age to Teresa. The widow was always very friendly to Teresa and to her father. When she saw them coming, she would hurry out to greet them. She would bring a water pitcher and something sweet to eat.

One day, Teresa's father said to her, "I know what I will do to make your life better, Teresa. I will marry the friendly widow who lives near town. She and her daughters will come and live here. That way, you will have company. You will have friends your own age and you will have help with the housework."

Teresa's heart was full of doubts. "You should not marry just for my sake," she said.

But her father had made up his mind. "The widow knows some rich people," he told her. "She makes sure that her daughters are dressed well. She takes them out to parties and dances. That is the kind of life that I want you to have."

So Teresa's father married the widow. But from the start, the marriage was unhappy. The widow had dearly wanted to remarry. But the home she now lived in was not to her liking. It was not big enough. It was too far from town. And her new husband did not make enough money to buy all the things she wanted. Teresa's new stepmother did not wish to help with household chores. She thought she and her daughters were too grand for such work. And so Teresa still had to do nearly all of the cooking, cleaning, washing, and mending. But now she had to do this work for five people, rather than for two.

Worst of all, Teresa's new stepsisters were very unkind to her. They treated her as if she were a servant. Laura and Lupe laughed at Teresa's plain clothes. They rolled their eyes when she spoke. Their mother never scolded them for this bad behavior. For she, too, saw Teresa as little more than a servant.

Teresa's father had always been away from the house a great deal. Now he had a nagging and unhappy wife at home. So he stayed away even more. One day, when he came home, he called his daughter and stepdaughters together. "I have a surprise for each of you," he said. And he gave each girl a half-grown lamb. "These lambs are all yours," he said. "You may sell them or keep them as you wish. These sheep will give lots of very fine wool. It will be good for spinning and weaving."

Teresa was very pleased with the gift. "Thank you, Father," she cried. And she hugged the lamb.

Laura and Lupe also said, "Thank you." But in truth they thought little of the gift they had been given. Neither girl was fond of animals. And they had no wish to do any spinning or weaving. The stepsisters sold their lambs at once. They used the money to buy fancy dresses. They would wear the dresses to the governor's ball in the summer.

Teresa wished that she too might have a new dress for the ball. But she could not bear to sell her lamb as her stepsisters had done. She found too much comfort in her new pet. She clipped the lamb's wool and set it aside. "When I have enough, I will weave a dress for myself," she thought.

During summer, Teresa's father went away for many weeks. He had to bring his flock down to the summer pasture. That pasture was at the bottom of a canyon. There the sheep could drink from the river and feed on grass that was still green. Teresa wished that she could go along and help with the sheep. But her stepmother would not allow this to happen.

     The Girl with the Little Gold Star

"You must stay and help here," her father said. "It is what your new mother wishes."

Teresa dreaded being left alone with her stepsisters and stepmother. But there was little she could do.

"At least, let me keep my lamb here with me," she begged. And her father allowed it.

With her father gone, Teresa's life was torture. Her only comfort was her pet lamb. Her stepsisters were crueler than ever. Their mother complained more than ever.

One day, the stepmother was complaining to her daughters about their food. "We live on a sheep farm," she moaned. "You would think we would at least have good meat to eat. But we haven't even had lamb chops in ages."

"Lamb chops sound delicious," said Lupe. "Let's have some for dinner."

"We can't. The flock is down in the valley," her mother reminded her.

"We still have one lamb here," said Laura. She meant, of course, Teresa's lamb.

The next day, Teresa went to the pasture looking for her lamb. She had brought a little treat for him. But she could see him nowhere. She wondered if he had got loose from his pen. She called and called, but the lamb was nowhere to be found. Finally, she rushed into the house. There, she found her stepmother cooking.

"Mother, have you seen my lamb?" she asked.

"What lamb do you mean?" her stepmother asked, stirring a pot.

"The lamb my father gave me," Teresa said. "The one that belongs to me."

"Now child, you must not be greedy," her stepmother said, licking a finger. "That lamb did not belong to you. It belonged to our whole family. And the rest of us had grown tired of beans and tortillas. We needed a change."

Teresa looked again at the pot on the stove. She smelled the meat roasting on the fire. "No!" she cried. "You didn't! You can't have!" And feeling sick, she ran from the kitchen.

After that, Teresa was lonelier than ever. With a heavy heart, she continued her daily chores. She hauled water and cleaned and mended. Meanwhile, Laura and Lupe spent their time planning for the governor's ball. Their talk was all of dresses and hairstyles. They guessed at the young men who might attend. They giggled about the governor's handsome son and dreamed that he might dance with them. Teresa asked her stepmother if she could go to the ball, too.

"You? At the governor's ball?" her stepmother laughed at her. "The finest people will all be there. You wouldn't know how to act. You've been little more than a housemaid your whole life. And, anyhow, what on Earth would you wear?"

It was true that Teresa had nothing fit to wear to the ball. And she had no money for new clothes. But she remembered that her father had wanted her to go to dances and parties. She wanted to go, too. She thought of the fine wool she had saved from the sheep shearing. She could spin it into yarn. Then she could weave it. She doubted she had enough to make a dress. Still, she would see. She began to prepare a tub of water so she could wash the wool for spinning. But as she was hauling the water, a hawk swooped down from the sky. It snatched the wool in its talons.

"Stop! Bring back my wool!" she cried.

But the hawk did not stop. It soared away over the hills and out of sight.

"Come back! Come back!" Teresa cried. But the hawk was gone. Teresa buried her head in her hands and began to sob. "Help me, somebody, help me," she cried as she sobbed.

Then suddenly she heard a voice on the wind. "Lift up your eyes. Look to the skies," the voice said. Teresa uncovered her eyes. She looked up. The hawk had returned and was circling above her head. It was holding something in its talons. Teresa squinted into the sun. She couldn't tell what the hawk was carrying.

The hawk swooped lower. It dropped the thing it had in its talons. A dress fell into Teresa's arms. The dress was made of soft, fine wool. And it was beautifully stitched. It was every bit as good as the fancy dresses that Laura and Lupe had bought. In fact, it was nicer.

Teresa was marveling at the dress, when she heard a voice again. "Lift up your eyes. Look to the skies," the voice said. Teresa looked up. The hawk was still there. It circled above her. Now it was holding something shiny in its beak. Teresa squinted into the sun. And as she did, the hawk dropped what it was holding. A shining star fell out of the sky and landed on Teresa's upturned forehead. And there it stuck fast. The hawk wheeled away. And Teresa was left wondering at what had happened.

Teresa said nothing about the hawk to anyone. She hid the dress. But there was no way she could hide the star.

"What is that thing you've got on your head?" her stepmother asked in an annoyed voice. "Take it off at once!" But Teresa couldn't take it off. And though they all scrubbed and scratched and prodded, the star held fast. "Then you must at least cover it up!" the stepmother said. And so Teresa was made to wear a scarf around her head at all times.

The evening of the governor's ball came. Laura and Lupe giggled and primped. Teresa had to help them get ready.

Teresa waited until the others were gone. Then she put on her lovely new dress. She took the scarf off of her head and brushed out her hair. Then she set out on foot for the dance.

It was very late by the time Teresa arrived at the governor's mansion. The doors were all closed. Teresa felt too nervous to enter. She knew her stepmother would be very angry. So she stood quietly out in the dark, looking in through a window and trying to get up her courage.

By now, the governor's son had danced with most of the young women at the party. He had even danced with Laura and Lupe. But he had not hit it off very well with any of these young ladies. In fact, he was feeling bored. All of a sudden, a light at the window caught his eye. Someone was standing there outside. It was a girl—a girl with a twinkling gold star on her forehead. The soft starlight lit up her lovely face. The governor's son felt almost as if he had met this girl before. He felt in his heart that she was someone special.

"Who are you?" he asked as his eyes met the eyes of the girl. "Why don't you come in?"

The girl at the window looked afraid. Then suddenly the light at the window was gone. The governor's son rushed outside. But the girl with the gold star was nowhere to be seen. "Who was that girl at the window?" he asked everyone at the party. "Did you see the girl with the gold star on her forehead?" But nobody else had seen her and nobody knew who she was.

The next day, the governor's son began to look for the girl with the little gold star. He rode all around the county, asking for her everywhere. But nobody knew where he could find her.

Finally, the governor's son came to the place where Teresa lived. Her father was still away and her stepmother answered the door. "Welcome, Señor!" said the stepmother happily. "You have come to see my lovely daughters, I suppose. They enjoyed the dance very much last night. Laura! Lupe!" she cried. "The governor's son is here to see you."

"I am glad your daughters enjoyed themselves," said the governor's son. "But I am looking for another young lady. I was hoping you could tell me where I might find her. I do not know her name. But she had a little gold star on her forehead."

Teresa's stepmother caught her breath sharply. Then she lied. "I have never seen such a girl," she said.

Just then, Teresa came up the path carrying a bucket of water. The governor's son turned and saw her. Her gold star was covered with a scarf. But he knew her face.

"It's you," he said in amazement. "You were the girl at the window. You were the girl with the little gold star."

"That is impossible," said the stepmother. "Teresa is just a servant. She was not at the ball. She has no gold star."

But Teresa was already removing the scarf from her head. She let it fall to the ground. The light of the little gold star poured out for all to see.

"I've found you!" cried the governor's son. And his face lit up with a smile that was almost as bright as the little gold star.

You know how the rest of this story goes. Teresa married the governor's son. They were very happy together. Teresa became a great lady, famous for her kindness and generosity. She was known throughout the countryside as Estrellita de Oro. (That is how you say "Little Gold Star" in Spanish.) All of her days, the gold star shone on Teresa's forehead. For what is inside of us—be it light or darkness—always finds a way to come out.

RED-TAILED HAWKS

- Hawks are raptors. That means they're hunting birds. They catch prey with their sharp claws, called talons.

- Red-tailed hawks are the most common hawks in North America. They live in most parts of the United States all year 'round.

- Red-tailed hawks are mostly brown, with reddish tail feathers. The feathers on their bellies are lighter colored. But not all red-tailed hawks look the same. Young hawks look different than adults. Hawks living in different places may look a little different. And the color of a hawk's feathers can change a little from season to season.

- Red-tailed hawks can be about two feet long. Their wingspan can be about four feet. But these birds are very lightweight, for their size. The largest red-tailed hawks only weigh about three pounds.

- What do red-tailed hawks like to eat? Rabbits, rats, mice, moles, snakes, and squirrels are all common meals. Red-tailed hawks also eat smaller birds such as blackbirds.

- Hawks have amazing eyesight. They are able to spot a mouse from about a half a mile away.

- In the past, many people tamed hawks. They used trained hawks for hunting. The hawks would catch small animals and bring them back to the hunter.

Be a Backyard Birder

Have you ever been bored in the backseat of a car on a long family trip? That's a great time to watch for red-tailed hawks. These big birds often can be seen soaring over fields or sitting on top of telephone poles.

EXTENSION ACTIVITY: HAWK EYES WALK

Concepts: animal behavior and species characteristics

For this activity, you will need:

pedometer(s)

realistically sized toy mouse or other item of similar size

open outdoor area

- Before undertaking the activity, read the **Feathered Facts File** on red-tailed hawks with the children. Or have children read the **Feathered Facts File** on their own.
- This is an outdoor/field trip activity. For this activity, you will need a half-mile of open space where you can walk with children. A flat field or long straight path will work. Alternatively, you may choose a hill site where you can walk with children up the hill for a half a mile. It is necessary that children will be able to view the place where they began the walk.
- Before beginning your walk, review what children know about hawks. Remind them that hawks have better vision than humans. Have children tell you why hawks need their exceptional vision. Remind children that red-tailed hawks are thought to be able to spot a mouse from about a half-mile away.
- Before beginning the walk, have one of the children place a toy mouse or similarly sized item on the ground (or on a rock, fence post, car roof, etc.) so that it will be visible as you walk away from it. If the mouse is placed on the ground, you may wish to add another marker such as a small flag, to give it additional visibility.
- Show the child or children how to use the pedometer(s), if necessary.
- Have one or more children use a pedometer to measure the distance as you walk away from the mouse.
- Have children check the distance periodically and note when a distance of 1/2 mile has been reached.
- At 1/2 mile, ask the children if any of them can still see the mouse. Remind them that they could still see it well enough to catch it and eat it if they were red-tailed hawks!

Chapter 9

Hummingbird

Appropriate for grades:

K-4

Reading level of story and fact file:

2.5

INTRODUCTION FOR PARENTS AND TEACHERS

The story in this chapter is based on an old, African American folkloric explanation for why hummingbirds always seem to be looking in flowers. Naturalist Ernest Ingersoll recorded this entertaining explanation in his 1923 book titled *Birds in Legend, Fable, and Folklore* (241).

Hummingbirds appear only in the folklore of the Americas, since they are only native to this part of the world. The ruby-throated hummingbird is the most familiar type of hummingbird that breeds east of the Mississippi River. Fifteen types of hummingbirds breed in the western portion of the United States. Facts in the **Feathered Facts File** pertain to hummingbirds in general. Much of the information about hummingbirds in this chapter, including that presented in the **Feathered Facts File,** is taken from Cornell University's *All About Birds* Web site. You can visit this site at http://www.allaboutbirds.org/guide/Ruby-throated_Hummingbird/id to learn about ruby-throated hummingbirds and other hummingbird species, find photographs of these birds, and play recordings of their wing noises and calls. You also can find many beautiful and fascinating photographs of hummingbirds in Robert Burton's *The World of the Hummingbird* (Kingston, Ontario: Firefly Books, 2001).

A recommended picture book about hummingbirds to share with children is *A Hummingbird's Life* by John Himmelman (New York: Children's Press, 2000).

STORY SHARING STRATEGY

Demonstrate the hummingbird's crazy flying with a hummingbird puppet or cutout during the story.

DISCUSSION OR WRITING PROMPT

This is a story about someone who gets in trouble by showing off. What is bad about showing off? Is it ever okay to show off? Explain.

How the Hummingbird Lost His Song

By Jennifer Kroll, based on African American folklore from the American South

All birds sing, right? Well, not all. Hummingbirds don't really have a song. They can make a few quiet chirps, and that's about it. Legend has it they used to be skilled at both singing and flying. Until one day . . .

Hummingbird was a real show-off. He was the smallest bird in the garden. But he had a beautiful singing voice. And he could fly like no other bird.

"Look at me go!" he sang out as he zigged here and zagged there.

"Bet you can't do this!" he twittered as he stopped in midair. His wings whirled around and around. They went so fast they were just a blur. Hummingbird's feathers sparkled in the light.

"Now you see me," he warbled, rising straight up into the air. "Now you don't!"

"Ooh! I want to sing like Hummingbird! I want to fly like Hummingbird!" chirped the little robins in their nest above the garden.

"You'll sing just fine," said their mother. She had returned with a worm. "And that's no way to fly. Twirling and whirling isn't good for a bird. Zigging and zagging will make you all mixed-up and dizzy. You need to keep your wits about you. Otherwise, a cat will catch you someday."

But the baby robins kept watching Hummingbird. "Wow, he's so cool," they said to each other. "I want to be like Hummingbird."

"Nonsense. That Hummingbird is just an accident waiting to happen," muttered their mother.

And she was right. The day came when an accident did happen. But it was not the one Mother Robin had imagined.

That day, Hummingbird was putting on quite a show. He was darting around above a colorful bed of flowers. All the while, he was singing at the top of his lungs.

"Watch me! I'm flying backwards!" sang Hummingbird.

"Ooh!" said the young robins. "Do it some more!"

Hummingbird circled the garden, flying backward and singing.

"And now for my newest trick!" called Hummingbird. "I am going to do a 60-mile-an-hour dive. And at the end of it, I will flip over. Watch and you will be amazed. I dare anyone else to try it!"

"Go, Hummingbird!" cheered the young robins.

Hummingbird rose up high into the sky. He zoomed toward the ground, singing loud. As he hit his high note, over he flipped. And as he did, something small and shiny fell out of his open mouth. Down it fell, into the bed of flowers.

"Wow! Cool!" The young robins were clapping and whistling.

But was something wrong?

Hummingbird had stopped zip-

ping and flipping. He hovered above the bed of flowers. He looked worried. He seemed to be trying to make noise. But the robins could hear no sound.

"Hummingbird can't seem to sing," one of them said.

"I saw something fall out when he flipped over," said another. "Maybe it was his song that fell out."

"I think it was," agreed a cardinal on the fence. "I think Hummingbird's song fell into one of those flowers."

Hummingbird must have thought so, too. For he had started searching through the flowers. He stuck his beak into a zinnia. Nothing there. He stuck his beak in a petunia. But his song was not there, either. On and on he looked.

And, to this day, Hummingbird is still looking through those flowers. He is looking and looking for his lost song.

HUMMINGBIRDS

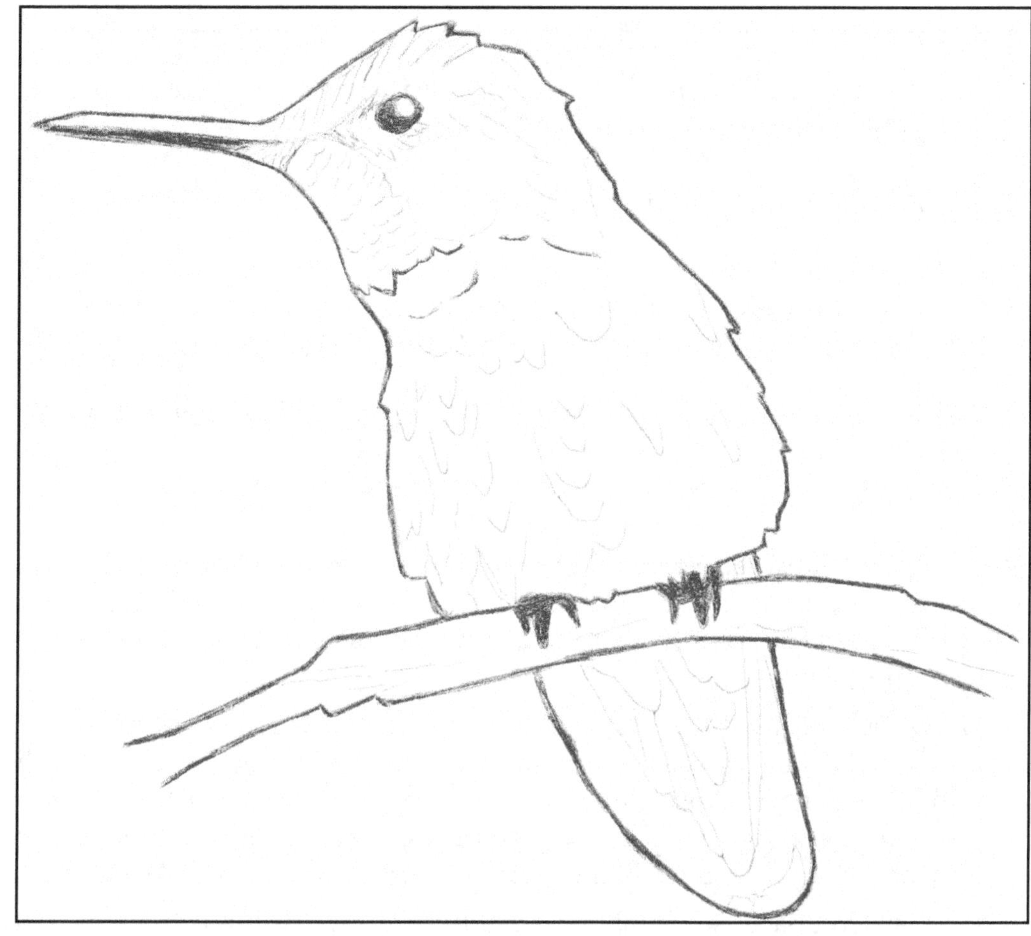

- One type of hummingbird common in the United States is the ruby-throated hummingbird. It is around 3½ inches long. That's about the length of a crayon.

- A hummingbird can fly backwards and sideways, as well as forward. It can stop and hover in mid-air like a helicopter. Then it can rise straight up or go straight down. Hummingbirds can do these tricks because they can move their wings around in a circle.

- Sometimes, male hummingbirds show off for females. They fly up high and then dive down at speeds up to 60 miles an hour.

- Hummingbirds don't hum. Their name comes from the humming sound their wings make when they fly. A hummingbird beats its wings about 80 times a second.

- Hummingbirds need a lot of energy to keep their wings (and hearts) beating so fast. They get much of this energy by sipping nectar from flowers. Hummingbirds also eat insects and tree sap. They eat up to three times their body weight in a day. Imagine if you had to do that!

- When they get cold, hummingbirds go into a state called *torpor.* Their hearts slow way down. This is the same thing that happens to animals that hibernate. But it can happen to a hummingbird that is just perched on a branch for the night. When sunlight warms the bird, he or she is ready to go again.

- Hummingbirds hang around flowers all day. But they have no sense of smell!

Be a Backyard Birder

Hummingbirds love the color red. To lure them to your yard, plant red flowers. Or put out a hummingbird feeder decorated with a red ribbon or red plastic trim.

EXTENSION ACTIVITY: HUMMINGBIRD GARDEN PLANS

Concepts: creating/using a map; sorting and arranging items by size and color; understanding the characteristics of bird species; planting and caring for plants

For this activity, you will need:

seed packets (or starter plants) for 5–12 different types of flowers

paper

pencils

yardstick or tape measure (optional)

crayons or markers (optional)

soil and planting tools (optional)

- Read the **Feathered Facts File** to children or have children read it independently. Point out the fact that hummingbirds drink nectar from flowers. Explain that hummingbirds especially like certain kinds of flowers. Describe how some people plant those kinds of flowers all together, creating hummingbird gardens.

- Show the children the seed packets or plants that you have purchased. Or have children help you pick out packets of seeds—or starter plants and bulbs—that would be appropriate for a hummingbird garden. Appropriate choices might include: cardinal flowers, snapdragons, hibiscus, bee balm, butterfly bush, zinnias, petunias, nasturtiums, hollyhocks, columbine, geraniums, azaleas, and cosmos. Hummingbirds are attracted to red, so make sure to include some red flowers.

- If a garden space is available for planting, show children the space. If appropriate, prompt the children to measure the space. Prompt the children to draw an outline of the garden space on a piece of paper. They can write in any measurements they've made.

- Alternatively, you may wish to make a handout for the children showing the general shape of the intended hummingbird garden. You can provide measurements on this garden map, if appropriate. You can also subdivide the garden bed into sections on the map.

- Talk about the seed packets (or starter plants or bulbs) with the children. Show the children how to read any information given on packets or tags, including the size they can expect the plants to reach when full grown.

- Have children work individually or in groups or teams to plan their hummingbird gardens. Set the following rules for the garden plans, if you wish: (1) Taller flowers must be in back of shorter flowers so that all flowers can be seen. (2) No plants of the same color should be next to each other. Prompt children to print the names of flowers (and their colors and sizes) in the desired spaces on the map.

- If possible, give children the opportunity to plant, or help plant, the garden(s) they've planned.

- Have children follow planting and care instructions that come with seeds or plants. You can also have students use the library and the Internet to find out more about the caring for the flowers they've planted.

Chapter 10

Loon

Appropriate for grades:

2–6

Reading level of story and fact file:

2.4

INTRODUCTION FOR PARENTS AND TEACHERS

The loon may be less familiar to American children than other birds represented in this collection. It is a bird of the far north that does not live happily in densely populated areas. For those who have lived near loons, their strange and haunting calls are unforgettable. These birds seem to have sparked the human imagination for thousands of years and folktales concerning loons are abundant. Both Eurasians and native peoples of North America have attributed magical powers to loons and related diving birds (Tate 30–35). Loons are capable of staying submerged for such a long time that humans have long imagined their dives as visits to another world beneath the waves. Evidence from ancient burial grounds in Alaska shows that native Alaskans once viewed these birds as escorts who helped the souls of the departed make their journey to the afterlife (Tate 33–34).

This chapter's tale, "The Gift of the Loon," is of Inuit/Eskimo origin. It is a tale that has been recorded many times in many varied versions. In some versions, the evil stepmother is an evil mother or grandmother. In most versions, she receives her punishment at the end of the story when her no-longer-blind son, stepson, or grandson kills her during a whaling expedition. The loon's mysterious power and desire to help the boy remain unexplained in most versions of the story. For alternative versions of the story, see the Works Consulted list.

71

Much of the information about loons in this chapter, including that presented in the **Feathered Facts File,** is taken from Cornell University's *All About Birds* Web site. You can visit this site to learn more about loons and find photographs of them. You can direct children to visit http://www.allaboutbirds.org/guide/Common_Loon/sounds, where they can listen to samples of loon calls.

A recommended picture book that depicts the life of loons is *Loon at Northwood Lake,* by Elizabeth Ring (Trudy, 1997).

STORY SHARING STRATEGY

The hero of this story is a blind child who regains sight. You may wish to have children shut or cover their eyes as they listen to the story, then open or uncover their eyes when the boy in the story regains his sight.

DISCUSSION OR WRITING PROMPT

Tell children: Until recently, people had not seen the ocean floor. Nobody knew what was down there. People imagined that diving birds like loons were making visits to another world down there. Use your imagination and draw a picture of another world down at the bottom of the sea. Write a description of what you've drawn or make up a story to go with the picture.

The Gift of the Loon

An Inuit/Eskimo legend as told by Jennifer Kroll

Once upon a time, in the far north, a blind boy lived with his father, stepmother, and little sister. The boy had been born without sight, but he was smart and strong and had a good heart. His father loved him well and took him hunting and fishing. In spite of his blindness, the boy was a good shot with a bow. If told where to aim, he almost always hit his mark.

One winter, when the days were dark and full of whirling snow, the boy's father became ill. A week later, he died. Then life became very hard for the boy. His stepmother had never loved him. And now, with two children to care for and food running low, she was bitter and angry. "You are useless!" she told the boy. "You will never be good for anything!" The boy felt his heart breaking every time he heard her say this.

At meal times, the stepmother always gave more to herself and to the little girl than she gave to her stepson. At night, she took all the warmest furs and blankets for herself and the girl. She gave the boy only old, thin, bug-eaten blankets.

The boy was miserable. He missed his father and was hungry all the time. But as time passed, he found a place where he could go to make himself feel better. He would sneak away to the edge of the lake. There, he would listen to the sad sound of a loon calling. The bird's voice seemed to speak the words that were in his own heart. He had learned from his father that loons dived deep, deep down into the water. He wondered what it was like down so deep. Was there another world down there? Was it happier than this one? Sometimes the boy would make up stories in his head about that other world down under the water. But he could only live in his imagination for so long. Then, he would have to return to the misery of his real life.

One day, when the whole family was at home, the boy heard footsteps outside. He heard a scratching at the window. Then, he heard his stepmother scream: "It's a polar bear! It's trying to get in!"

The boy knew a thin window made of ice would not keep out a hungry bear for long. He scrambled to find his bow and arrows. Then he ran to the door. "Quick!" he cried to his stepmother. "Aim the bow at the bear and I will shoot it!" The stepmother aimed and the boy shot. He knew at once it had been a good shot. He could hear the bear cry out and land with a heavy thump in the snow.

But the stepmother did not praise the shot or thank the boy. Instead, she yelled, "You useless boy! You've missed the bear! He got away! You've shot my favorite dog, instead!"

The boy felt confused. Then he guessed that his stepmother was lying. Later that day, the hut was filled with the delicious smell of cooking bear meat. Now the boy *knew* that his stepmother was lying. The meat of the big bear would feed the family for weeks. Yet, at mealtime, the boy found only a little broth set before him. "Thanks to you, this is all we have to eat," his stepmother said.

The boy's sister hated to see her brother so hungry. But she was very young and afraid to speak out. Instead, she hid most of her dinner and saved it. And later, when the stepmother was sleeping, she gave the dinner to her brother. In whispers, she told him what the stepmother had done.

The next day, the stepmother cooked more bear meat. But she gave the boy only broth again. In the middle of the day, the boy sneaked down to the lake. He listened to the loon crying and could hold back his tears no longer. He was so frustrated and angry that he cried and cried. As he cried, he heard the bird coming closer and closer. Finally, he heard a voice.

"Let me help you."

The boy stopped crying. "Who are you?" he asked.

"I am the loon," said the voice. "I have been watching you for a long time. I know how unhappy you are. I want to help."

"How can you help?" asked the boy, amazed.

"The water of this lake is very pure," said the loon. "If you dive down deep with me, it will wash your eyes clean. You will be able to see again."

"How can I dive with you?" asked the boy. "You go much farther down than any person can. You hold your breath much longer than a boy ever could."

"Climb on my back," said the loon. "I will not let you drown. I will bring you up again when you need air."

The boy did not understand how he could climb on the back of a bird so small. But, when he reached out he found that the bird had grown. Or perhaps he had magically become smaller, for he fit right on the back of the bird. He clasped his arms around the bird's neck.

"Ready?" said the loon.

"Yes," said the boy. And the loon dove.

Down, down, down went the boy. He felt the water pressing against his body and washing over his eyes. Deeper and deeper he went. He was running out of air. He began to panic. But then, the loon pushed back up toward the surface. The boy came gasping out into the air again.

And, for the first time in his life, the boy saw light.

"What do you see?" the loon asked.

"Light," cried the boy. "I can see light!"

"We will dive again so that you can see more," said the loon.

And down they went. Down, down, down where the water pressed against him and his lungs felt that they would burst.

This time, when they came back up, the boy saw shapes and shadows. Everything was a blur, but the boy was amazed.

"What do you see?" the loon asked.

"Shapes," cried the boy. "I can see shapes!"

"We're almost there," said the loon. "Hold on tight." And they plunged back down into the water again.

This time, when he came back up, the boy could see everything. And his sight was not just like yours or mine. He could see like a bird—things far, far away. He looked far across the lake and saw the smoke rising from the fires of the people who lived there. He saw children playing there on the other side. The children were happy and laughing.

"What can you see now?" asked the loon, as the boy slid off and scrambled ashore.

"I can see everything!" he cried. "I can see all the way across to the village on the other side of the lake!"

"The water has washed your eyes clean," said the loon.

"Thank you!" cried the boy. "How can I repay you?"

But with a splash, the loon had already disappeared.

And after that, what happened to the blind boy who had been cured by a loon?

Some people say he returned to live with his stepmother. He bided his time. Then later, he got even. He tricked his stepmother so that she drowned while they were out hunting whales.

But I don't think that's what happened. I think the boy never saw his stepmother again. He returned to the hut only long enough to take one last look at his old life. With disgust, he saw the dirty, bug-eaten blankets on the floor. He saw the piles of bear meat. He saw his little sister taking her nap. Gently, he woke her.

"I'm leaving now," he said. "I'm not coming back. Do you want to come with me?"

"Yes," said the girl, as she rubbed her eyes and sat up. "But where will we go?"

"There is a place across the lake," said the boy. "I've seen it with my own eyes."

And the boy took his sister by the hand. Together, they left the hut. Down by the water, they found their father's old fishing boat. The boy put the boat into the water and he put his sister into the boat.

Then the boy pushed off.

He never looked back.

   The Gift of the Loon

COMMON LOONS

- These water birds are larger than a mallard duck and smaller than a goose. Their red eyes help them see under water.
- Some people think a male loon's cry sounds like laughter.
- Loons don't like to be crowded. They live on wooded lakes. Usually, a lake will have only one pair of loons living on it.
- Loons were born to swim and dive and are very clumsy on land. They sometimes even fall over when they try to run.
- Most birds have hollow bones. Loons have solid bones and heavy bodies. The weight of their bodies helps them dive. It makes it hard for them to take off, though! Loons need a 100- to 600-foot runway of water in order to take off into the sky. Once in the air, loons can travel at 75 miles an hour.
- What's on the menu when loons go for lunch? Fish, usually. Loons also eat frogs, insects, leeches, crayfish, and mollusks such as clams.
- Loon moms and dads take turns sitting on the eggs. Baby loons sometimes ride on their parents' backs.
- The loon is the state bird of Minnesota.

Be a Backyard Birder

It's fun to watch diving loons. You can use a watch to time how long a loon stays under water. Loons usually stay down between 8 and 60 seconds. But if in danger, they can stay down much longer.

EXTENSION ACTIVITY: ADAPTED FOR DIVING

Concepts: characteristics of animals, adaptation

For this activity, you will need:

a clear glass or plastic container such as a fish tank

water

two straws (preferably of different colors, wider work better)

duct tape or other strong tape

scissors

fine sand

a measuring cup with a narrow pour spout

- Gather and prepare materials. Tape closed one end of each of the straws. Fill the tank with water.
- Share the story and Feathered Facts File with children. Bring children's attention to the fact that the bones of loons are solid, while the bones of many other birds are hollow on the inside. Ask: "Why do you think loons have solid bones? How does having solid bones help them?" Note children's responses.
- Say: "We are going to do an experiment about birds' bones. Here are two straws. We will pretend they are bones inside of two birds. This bone is inside of a loon, so it needs to be solid. To make it solid, let's fill it up with sand." Allow children to fill one of the straws, then tape the end closed securely. Make sure that the straw is as full as possible and has no air pocket inside.
- Say: "Let's pretend this straw is a bone inside another bird, such as a sparrow. It is hollow on the inside." Have children tape closed the hollow straw.
- Have a child or children hold the two straws so that they are both just above the water, pointed down. Instruct other children to watch carefully and note which straw goes down farther into the water.
- Have the child or children thrust the two straws down into the water simultaneously.
- Ask: "Which straw got the farthest down into the water?" Note that the filled straw, your solid loon bone, went farther down into the water before floating up.
- Ask again: "So how does having solid bones help a loon?" Children will respond that it helps the loon dive farther down in the water to catch fish/find food.
- Ask the children how having hollow/light bones might help other kinds of birds that don't dive for food. Cue children to realize that light bones/bodies are useful for flying. Remind children of how difficult it is for loons to get into the air. Have them think of the birds they usually see in their own yards, birds that can get off the ground very quickly and easily.
- You may wish to share the term *adaptation* with the children. Say: "When an animal's body changes so that it can survive better in the place where it lives we call that an adaptation." Tell the children that solid bones are an adaptation that helps loons live in the water and hunt for food there. You may also wish to discuss the placement of a loon's legs as an adaptation. These birds' legs are placed so far back on their bodies that they cannot walk easily on land. But the placement of their legs makes their bodies more streamlined so that they can dive deeper with less water resistance.

Chapter 11

Mallard Duck

Appropriate for grades:

K-4

Reading level of story and fact file:

2.3

INTRODUCTION FOR PARENTS AND TEACHERS

Mallards are the most common species of ducks in the northern hemisphere. These are the ducks we North Americans most often see on lakes, ponds, and rivers. Many children may already know that green-headed mallards are full-grown males and the more muted brown mallards are females and young ducks. Some children even may have had the experience of watching mallard ducklings at a local park, pond, or lake.

The story in this chapter, a tale from the Eastern Cherokee, focuses on the antics of a rabbit who decides to try his hand at duck hunting. The Mr. Rabbit of the tale is similar to the Brer Rabbit character that one encounters in the famous Uncle Remus stories of Joel Chandler Harris. In fact, a number of the Uncle Remus stories are remarkably similar to Eastern Cherokee folktales. (For an Eastern Cherokee version of the famous "Tar Baby" story, see *Cherokee Animal Tales* by George F. Scheer, p. 47.) Stories of a trickster rabbit figure clearly passed back and forth between Cherokee Indians and the slaves and free people of West African heritage living with and near them.

Much of the information about mallards in this chapter, including that presented in the **Feathered Facts File,** is taken from Cornell University's *All About Birds* Web site. You can visit this site at http://www.allaboutbirds.org/guide/Mallard/id to learn about the life

79

history of mallards, see photographs of these ducks, and play recordings of their calls and quacks.

A recommended picture book about the mallard duck life cycle is *Mallard Duck at Meadow View Pond* by Wendy Pfeffer (Smithsonian Backyard, 2001). The classic picture book, *Make Way for Ducklings,* by Robert McCloskey (Viking Press, 1941), also depicts a family of mallard ducks.

STORY SHARING STRATEGY

Use puppets to tell the story. You will need a rabbit, an otter, and a duck puppet. You may wish to have some kind of a line or string to use as Mr. Rabbit's lasso. Attach Mr. Rabbit to the end of the line, fly him around the room, and drop him into a (clean) wastebasket or an empty box at the point in the story when Mr. Rabbit falls into the hollow tree. Have children play the roles of the boy, girl, and father at the end of the story.

DISCUSSION OR WRITING PROMPT

After reading, ask children if they found the story funny. Ask them what was funny about it. Ask if they found the idea of a rabbit hunting for ducks funny. Talk about how hunting is not something a rabbit would really do. Rabbits are plant eaters. Have children brainstorm ideas for other funny stories in which an animal character does something that type of animal would not normally do or be good at. For instance, you might suggest a story in which an owl stays up all day, a cat plays fetch, or a snail runs a race. Have children write or tell their mixed-up animal stories.

Mr. Rabbit Goes Duck Hunting

A folktale from the Eastern Cherokee as told by Jennifer Kroll

Mr. Rabbit was out walking along the stream with his friend Ms. Otter.

"Your fur is looking quite lovely today," Mr. Rabbit said to Ms. Otter. "Indeed, I've never seen it looking quite so silky before."

"How kind of you to say so," said Ms. Otter.

"What's your secret?" asked Mr. Rabbit. He looked down at his own fur. It was not as shiny as he would have liked.

"I think it's my diet," said Ms. Otter. "I think it's the ducks. My mother always said they make the coat gleam."

"The ducks?" asked Mr. Rabbit.

"Yes," said Ms. Otter. "I mostly eat fish, you know. I eat lots of clams and crayfish, too. But every so often, I also like to catch a duck and eat it."

Mr. Rabbit looked downstream toward the pond. Some mallard ducks were swimming around there. They were talking quite loudly to one another. They didn't look very tasty—or very easy to catch. "How do you catch a duck?" Mr. Rabbit asked Ms. Otter.

"It's simple," said Ms. Otter. "I swim under water, holding my breath. I sneak up on a duck and grab its legs. Then I just pull it under. I'm very good at duck hunting," she said proudly. "But then again, I'm an otter. We otters have skills that a rabbit like yourself could never hope to have."

This was surely true. But Mr. Rabbit was the sort of fellow who did not like to be one-upped at anything. "It can't be very hard to catch a duck," he scoffed. "I'm sure I could catch one quite easily if I wanted to."

"You could, could you?" Ms. Otter laughed. "Then show me. Go catch a duck right now."

Mr. Rabbit looked at the ducks again. They looked big and pretty tough. He gazed at the pond water. It looked murky and cold. He shivered just thinking about climbing into it. "I'm not very hungry right now," he said to Ms. Otter. "I think I'll catch a duck later."

Ms. Otter laughed again. "You're just saying that. You won't catch one later. You could never catch a duck. I bet you can't even swim," she said.

That did it. Mr. Rabbit could indeed swim. It wasn't something he liked to do. But he could swim. And how hard could it really be to catch a duck? If someone like Ms. Otter could do it, it must be a breeze. "All right, then," he said to his friend. "I guess I'm hungry for a duck after all. I'll show you what a fine hunter I am. But we rabbits hunt our ducks in a little different way than you otters do. The first thing I need for duck hunting is a bit of rope. Watch and learn," he said to the otter.

Mr. Rabbit rambled up the bank toward a tree with vines hanging from it. He gnawed off a length of vine. Then he looped the vine around and tied it, making a lasso. He tested his lasso. It seemed like it would work. He put the vine lasso into his mouth and plunged into the pond.

The pond water got into Mr. Rabbit's nose and mouth and ears. It matted down his nice soft fur. Mr. Rabbit wanted to be like Ms. Otter. He wanted to swim under the water and sneak up on a duck. But he couldn't quite get the hang of that sort of swimming. Every time Mr. Rabbit put his face under the water, he came up coughing and spluttering and splashing. He made a huge racket. And pretty soon most of the ducks on the pond were looking at him. Some of them were laughing. "What is that silly rabbit over there trying to do?" they asked each other. They didn't seem worried about being hunted by Mr. Rabbit. Not at all.

Mr. Rabbit splashed over toward a large brown duck.

"Hello," she said, as he approached. "What are you doing 'way out here?"

Mr. Rabbit wanted to say something fierce-sounding. But the lasso was in his mouth. So what he said came out like, "Umph humphing furruss."

The duck laughed. Then she stuck her head under water to grab a mouthful of plants. When she came up with her mouthful, Mr. Rabbit saw his chance. He took aim and flung his lasso over the duck's head.

"There!" he cried. (He could talk better now, because he no longer had the lasso in his mouth.) "I've caught you!"

"What exactly do you think you're doing?" asked the duck.

"I've caught you!" Mr. Rabbit repeated. "You've been hunted!"

"Get this thing off of me!" the duck quacked. "Rabbits don't hunt ducks, you nutcase!"

"This one does," said Mr. Rabbit, proudly. "I'm not just *any* rabbit. I'm a very special rabbit. I like to do things that other rabbits don't do."

"Oh you do, do you?" snorted the duck. "Then how about going for a little fly? Most rabbits don't fly. But since you're a special rabbit and all that." And the duck flapped her wings and took off from the surface of the pond.

     Mr. Rabbit Goes Duck Hunting

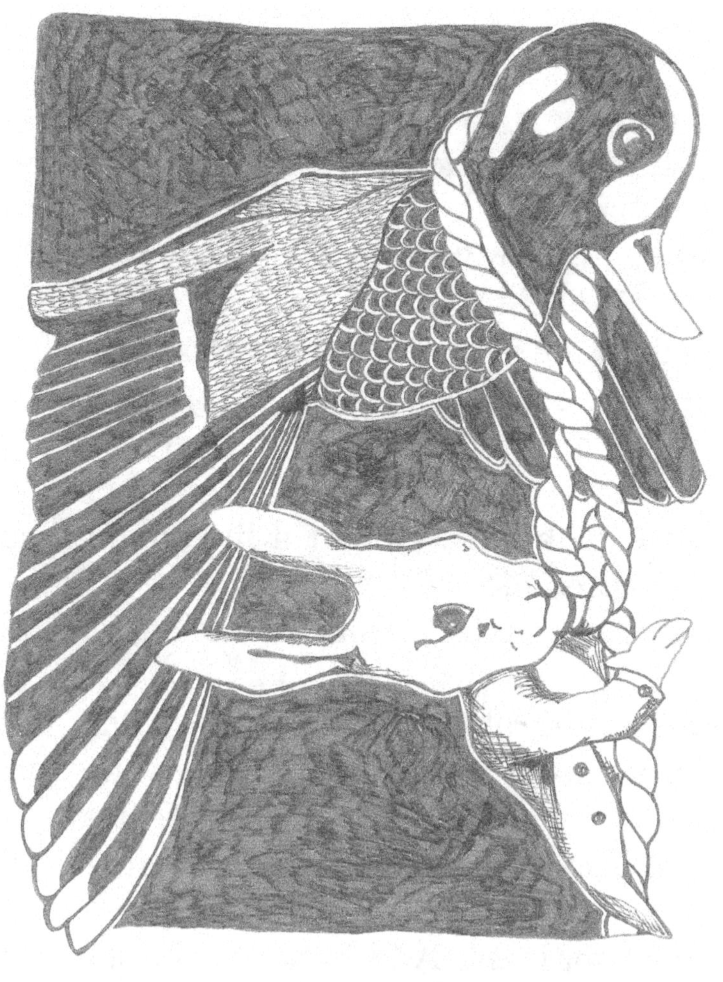

Mr. Rabbit realized what was happening too late. He could have dropped his end of the lasso and stayed in the water. But by the time he thought of that, he was high above the pond. He was dangling from the end of a rope that was looped around the duck's neck. He could see Ms. Otter down below. She was rolling on the ground laughing. The other ducks were looking up at him and laughing, too. The pond and ducks were getting farther and farther away. "Please take me back down," he begged the duck. "I promise I will never bother you again."

"Humph," said the duck. "I don't think I'm ready to land just yet. It's such a nice day for flying. But feel free to let go anytime you want. That will get you back down in a hurry." And she took off over the woods.

Mr. Rabbit didn't want to let go. He didn't want to get back down in that much of a hurry. But after a while, he didn't have much choice. He could only hold on so long. Then his paws slipped and down he fell.

Mr. Rabbit was a silly fellow. But he was also a lucky fellow. And as luck would have it, he landed inside a hollowed-out tree that was filled with leaves. The leaves cushioned his fall. He had some bumps and bruises. But, mostly, he was just fine . . . except that he was stuck. Mr. Rabbit couldn't get out of that hollow tree stump for quite a while. It might have even been a day or two, or even longer.

Finally, he heard the voices of some children playing nearby.

"Ah! Here's my chance!" thought Mr. Rabbit to himself. "These children can get me out." And he began to sing a little song. It went something like this:

Cut a hole and you will see
The magical creature inside this tree.

"What's that?" the little girl asked the little boy. "It sounds like that tree over there is singing!"

"Something's inside the tree," said the little boy. "It is a magic creature. It is telling us to cut a hole. Listen!"

And Mr. Rabbit sang again:
Cut a hole and you will see
The beautiful creature inside this tree.
"Quick! Let's go get Father to cut a hole!" said the little girl. "I want to see the beautiful creature inside the tree!"

Mr. Rabbit waited. And in not too long, the brother and sister were back. They had brought their father.

"Now where is this tree you were telling me about?" asked the father.

And Mr. Rabbit sang again, as loud as he could:
Cut a hole and you will see
The wonderful creature inside this tree.
So the father cut a hole in the tree with his ax. He cut a little hole. The rabbit saw the little girl put her eye up to the hole.

"I still can't see the creature. Please keep cutting," said the little girl. And the father cut some more.

Now the hole was just big enough for a thin rabbit to squeeze through. And Mr. Rabbit was quite thin, as he hadn't eaten for a while. So through the hole he squeezed. He popped out and dashed away as fast as his rabbit feet would carry him. All that the boy and the girl and the father saw was a streak of brown and white fur.

Mr. Rabbit didn't stop running until he got home. And as he ran, he thought to himself: "I can't catch ducks like an otter. And I can't fly like a duck. But I'm good at what I'm good at. I sure am fast. And nobody has gotten out of more close scrapes than me."

And—you know what? That just might be the truth.

MALLARDS

- The world today is full of lots of kinds of ducks. Many look very different from mallards. But scientists think almost all ducks alive today are descended from mallards.

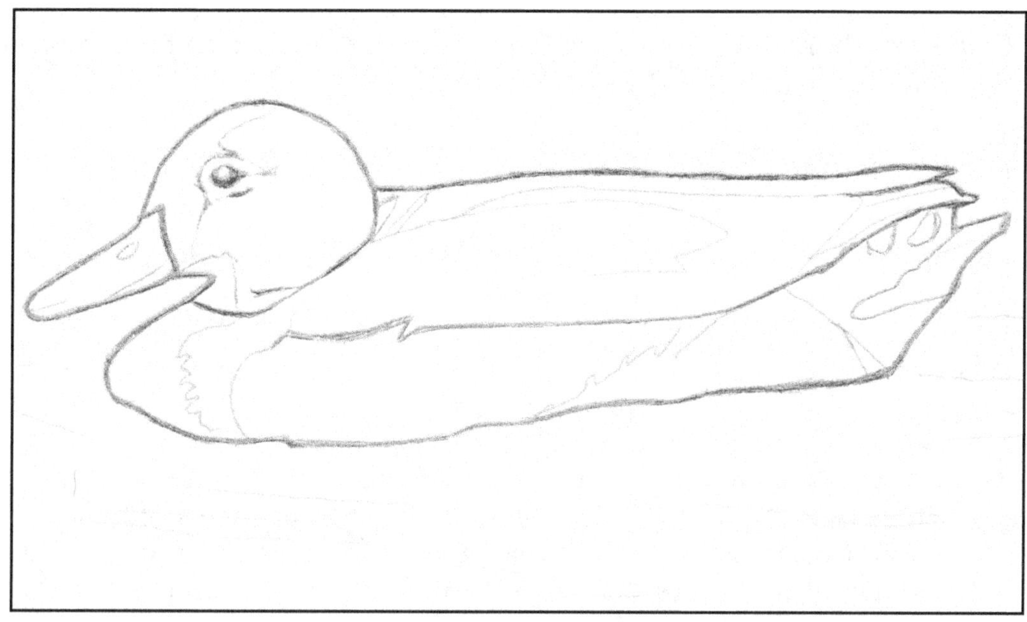

- It is easy to tell male and female mallards apart. Males have a showy green head. Females are brown. Why are males and females such different colors? Being brown helps females stay hidden. This is helpful when females are caring for eggs and baby ducklings.

- Mallard ducklings know how to swim when they are born. Mother ducks lead their babies to water almost at once.

- Mallards are dabbling ducks. This means they stick their heads under water and their tails in the air when they eat.

- What do mallards find to eat under the water? They find seeds, water plants, insects, small fish, fish eggs, frogs, tadpoles, and snails.

- Mallards don't need a running start in order to fly. They can take off from the surface of the water—straight up into the air.

Be a Backyard Birder

It's fun to feed ducks at the local park or pond. But don't feed them bread. Too much bread can pollute water, cause disease, and shorten ducks' lives. Instead, try corn, oats, birdseed, or frozen peas. Grapes are another good choice. (Make sure you cut them in half.)

EXTENSION ACTIVITY: DUCK DUCK GAMES

Concepts: characteristics of mallard ducks, animal habitats, migration, impact of human behavior on habitats and species

For this activity, you will need:

pencil	a container such as a bag, basket, hat, or jar
paper	poker chips (or substitute)
scissors	

- Young children love to play "Duck Duck Goose." Here's another duck game to play with children. It will help them learn about mallard ducks and the impact of human actions on animals and the environment. Prepare for the game by cutting out strips of paper. Print the following and similar scenarios on the strips of paper: "You find a pond with lots of tasty water plants." "The pond freezes over early." "A fox is prowling around the pond." "People throw litter in the pond." "Lots of tasty tadpoles are swimming in your pond." "People use motorboats and jet skis on your pond." "A law is passed to keep motorboats off the pond." "A man dumps oil in the pond after changing the oil in his truck." "The pond water dries up in late summer." "The woods near the pond get cut down and houses are built there." "Winter ends and you migrate back to your favorite pond."

- Fold up slips of paper and put them in a container such as a bag, basket, hat, or jar.

- If four or more children are present, divide the children into teams. Give each team four bingo chips to start with. Place the rest of the chips in a pile or in a second container. You may substitute some other type of item (treats, small rubber ducks, etc.) for bingo chips, if you wish.

- Tell the children that they should pretend they are ducks, or flocks of ducks, living on ponds. Show them the container with the slips of paper in it. Tell them that each paper slip describes something that happens that affects the lives of ducks. Any time they pick out an event that is good for ducks, they get to take another bingo chip. Any time they pick out an event that is bad for ducks, they must put back a bingo chip. The winning child or team will be the one with the most chips when the slips are gone.

- Have children or teams take turns picking event slips from the container. Have a child read the selected event aloud, or you can read it for the child. Have children discuss whether the event is good for ducks or bad for ducks and why. If the event is good for ducks, prompt the child or team to take a bingo chip from the pile or bag. If the event is bad for ducks, prompt the child or team to return a bingo chip to the pile or bag.

- Have children continue until all slips have been selected and read. Then have children count up their bingo chips. Declare a winning player or team.

Chapter 12
Meadowlark

Appropriate for grades:

K-4

Reading level of story and fact file:

2.7

INTRODUCTION FOR PARENTS AND TEACHERS

Meadowlarks make their homes in prairies and open fields. Farmers are often fond of these yellow-breasted birds because they eat insects that can harm crops. Bigfoot Bird of the Cherokee folktale that follows is a meadowlark. The mother bird of the story may also be a meadowlark. Female meadowlarks, like the mother bird character, build their nests on the ground and take sole responsibility for tending eggs and young. A bit of modern farm machinery has been added to the version of *Bigfoot Bird* that follows.

You can visit Cornell University's *All About Birds* Web site at http://www.allabout birds.org/guide/Western_Meadowlark/id to learn about western meadowlarks and their eastern meadowlark cousins, find photographs of these birds, and play recordings of their song and calls.

STORY SHARING STRATEGY

Use plastic Easter eggs as a prop while reading or telling this story. Create a nest out of a twisted towel or a bowl and place at least six eggs inside. Act out the part of the story where Bigfoot Bird carries the eggs to safety, two by two.

Alternatively, have children recreate the story as a play, using the eggs and nest props. Children not playing the roles of Bigfoot Bird, Butterfly, or Mother Bird can be enlisted to make scary motor sounds at the point in the story when the eggs are threatened.

DISCUSSION OR WRITING PROMPT

Say: In this story, Bigfoot Bird doesn't like his feet. He sees his big feet as a bad thing. But the big feet turn out to be useful and a good thing. Do you have something about yourself that you don't like? Make up a story in which that bad thing turns out to be a good thing.

Bigfoot Bird

A Cherokee folktale as told by Jennifer Kroll

Bigfoot Bird was a meadowlark. He lived in a sunshiny meadow full of tall waving grass and lovely wildflowers. Bigfoot Bird loved his meadow home. He loved the sunshine and the wildflowers. But he especially loved the tall grass because he could hide in it. Bigfoot Bird stayed hidden most of the time. You see, he didn't want anyone to get a look at his big feet.

Meadowlarks don't usually have huge feet. But this one did. When his body stopped growing, his feet kept on. And now they looked like they were about five sizes too big for the rest of him. Bigfoot Bird hated his big feet. He worried that other birds would laugh at them. And so he kept hidden.

Still, other animals knew that Bigfoot Bird was there. They knew because they could hear him singing.

"What a lovely song you sing," said Butterfly to Bigfoot Bird one day. "Why don't you go perch on that fence post over there? Then everyone will be able to hear you even better. And we can see you better, too."

"I'd rather stay down here in the grass," said Bigfoot Bird. "I don't want anyone to see me."

"Why?" asked Butterfly.

"Because I'm ashamed of my ugly feet," said Bigfoot Bird. "See how big they are?" And he held up a foot so Butterfly could see.

"I don't see what the big deal is," said Butterfly with a shrug. "Your feet aren't ugly. Different isn't the same as ugly. Your feet look fine to me. In fact, I bet one of these days your big feet will come in handy."

And Butterfly was right.

On the other side of the road from the meadow was a cornfield. A mother bird had made her nest on the ground there. Now her eggs were almost ready to hatch. But something else was about to happen, too. The farmer who owned the field had come. He was there to harvest the corn. The mother bird heard the sound of a motor. She could see the big, noisy combine harvester. It was still far away. But soon it would reach her nest. Her eggs would surely be crushed.

"Oh no! Oh no!" the mother bird cried in alarm. "My babies will be hurt!"

"What's the matter?" asked the Butterfly. She happened to be fluttering by.

"The farmer has come to harvest the corn," said the mother bird to the Butterfly. "Before the day ends, my eggs will surely be crushed. I need to move them to safety, but I can't lift them. Will you help me move my eggs?"

"I can't move your eggs," said the Butterfly. "But I know someone who may be able to help you." And the Butterfly fluttered off to find the Bigfoot Bird.

Bigfoot Bird was singing in the meadow. Butterfly couldn't see him, but she could hear him. "Bigfoot Bird, come quickly!" called Butterfly. "A mother bird needs your help. Her nest is in the cornfield. The farmer is coming with his noisy machine. The eggs will be crushed. They need to be moved to safety."

"But how can I help?" asked the Bigfoot Bird.

"Use your feet!" said the Butterfly.

And that is what Bigfoot Bird did. He came flying up out of hiding. And two by two, he carried those eggs away from the cornfield. With his big feet, he set the eggs carefully down in the meadow.

"Thank you! Thank you!" cried the mother bird to Bigfoot Bird. "Thank goodness for those wonderful big feet of yours!"

Now Bigfoot Bird isn't ashamed of his feet anymore. In fact, he's proud of them. He doesn't hide in the grass anymore. He sits up on the fencepost where everyone can see him. He puffs out his pretty yellow chest as he sings. And his beautiful song can be heard all over the meadow.

   Bigfoot Bird

MEADOWLARKS

- Meadowlarks have bright yellow throats, chests, and bellies. From the front, they look like they are wearing a black, V-shaped necklace.
- The western meadowlark is the state bird of six states! The states are Kansas, Nebraska, Montana, Oregon, North Dakota, and Wyoming. The cardinal is the only bird that is state bird for more states.
- Meadowlarks build their nests on the ground. They use dried grass and bark. Sometimes they build a little roof to cover the nest. Then they build a tunnel for going in and out.
- Mother meadowlarks try to keep their nest spots secret. They walk away from their nests before they fly up into the air. They also carry grass to a spot that is not their nest spot. They do this to try to fool predators.
- Most farmers like meadowlarks. These birds eat insect pests that can harm crops.
- The number of meadowlarks has gone down a lot in the last 50 years. That's because meadowlarks are losing the land that they call home. Meadowlarks live in open fields full of wild grasses. People mow these prairies. They poison "weeds." They build houses and shopping centers. Then meadowlarks have no place to nest and no food to eat.

Be a Backyard Birder

Keep a corner of your yard wild. Help your family plant flowers and grass that are native to where you live. You are almost sure to get lots of animal visitors. And many of your visitors will be birds.

EXTENSION ACTIVITY: FEATHER FUNCTIONS

Concepts: types of bird feathers and their functions; sorting objects by type; making a graph or bar chart (optional)

For this activity, you will need:

feathers, preferably an assortment of different types

paper (optional)

pencils (optional)

markers or crayons (optional)

- Have children collect feathers they find on sidewalks, in parks, fields, on the school ground, or on lawns. Or start your own feather collection and share what you find with the children.
- Tell children that not all bird feathers have the same job. Have children look at a collection of feathers. Ask them what jobs they think the different feathers do for the birds they come from.
- Tell children some feathers are called downy feathers. Ask which feathers in the collection are downy feathers. These are small and fluffy. They do not "zip up" as other feathers do. Have children guess the function of these feathers. Explain that these feathers help a bird stay warm.
- Tell children that the longest bird feathers are tail feathers and flight (wing) feathers. See if children can pick out tail and flight feathers. Tail feathers differ from flight feathers in that they are generally longer and more symmetrical. Their ends are more squared off. Give children a chance to examine tail and flight feathers. Have them point to the place where the feathers attach to the bird. Allow the children to play with the feathers, zipping and unzipping them.
- The final type of feathers you may have in your collection are contour feathers. These are smaller and rounder than flight and tail feathers. These feathers help the bird stay warm and protected from rain, snow, wind, and objects. They also act as sunblock. And they give the bird its general coloring and look.
- Ask the children if they know why birds lose their feathers. Explain that birds lose feathers so that they can replace old, worn-out feathers with new ones. Most birds lose their feathers twice a year. This process is called *molting*.
- Have children group the feathers in the collection together by function. Then challenge them to group the feathers together in other ways, such as by size or color.
- If desired, pass out pencils, paper, and markers or crayons. Have children make a graph or bar chart that represents the total group of feathers. The chart might, for instance, show numbers of feathers cross-referenced with feather function or color.

Chapter 13

Mockingbird

Appropriate for grades:

K-4

Reading level of story and fact file:

2.8

INTRODUCTION FOR PARENTS AND TEACHERS

The featured story in this chapter is adapted from a Mayan folktale. The story is a classic underdog-makes-good story, very much in the same vein as Cinderella. The tale emphasizes the mockingbird's singing skill. Facts in the fact file section of the chapter pertain to the northern mockingbird, a species common throughout the United States, Mexico, and parts of Central America.

Much of the information about mockingbirds in this chapter, including that presented in the **Feathered Facts File,** is taken from Cornell University's *All About Birds* Web site. You can visit this site at http://www.allaboutbirds.org/guide/Northern_Mockingbird/id to learn about the life history of mockingbirds, see photographs of them, and listen to recordings of their songs and calls.

STORY SHARING STRATEGY

Tell children that this is a story about a bird that takes singing lessons and then gives a recital. Ask children if they know what a recital is. Have children share their experiences with lessons and recitals. Have them describe their feelings about performing in (or watching other children perform in) recitals.

DISCUSSION OR WRITING PROMPT

Say: The cardinal girl was lip-synching (or beak-synching) at her recital. Sometimes real human performers do this, too. They pretend to sing by just mouthing the words. Do you think it is ever okay for performers to lip-synch on TV or at concerts? Why or why not?

The Mockingbird's First Recital

A Mayan folktale as told by Jennifer Kroll

One day, the rich cardinal was talking to his wife. "I would like our daughter to become a famous singer," he said. "I'm going to buy her some singing lessons."

"But dear," said the cardinal's wife. "Does our daughter *want* to take singing lessons? She doesn't show much interest in singing."

The cardinal did not listen to his wife. "I know just the teacher we should get," he went on. "All the finest families have been hiring Dr. Blackbird. His lessons cost a lot of money. But if Dr. Blackbird can make our daughter a star, it will be worth it."

And so the rich cardinal got the famous teacher to come. "Make sure you do what your teacher asks," the cardinal told his daughter. "Practice hard. I'm paying a lot for these lessons, you know."

The cardinal girl wanted to please her father. She really did. But her mother was right. She just didn't have much interest in singing. And on top of that, she didn't have much talent for it, either. At first, she tried to do everything that Dr. Blackbird asked. But she quickly grew tired of practicing. She longed to be out playing with her friends. Her practices grew shorter and shorter. Then she started showing up late for lessons. Soon she was skipping her lessons altogether.

Now, one of the family's maids was a mockingbird girl. The mockingbird was poor. She could only afford to dress in plain gray feathers. But she had what the cardinal's daughter did not have. She had a talent and love for singing. In secret, she listened in on the singing lessons. She listened to what Dr. Blackbird told the young cardinal. In secret, she practiced. Soon her voice was amazing. But almost nobody knew this. Only the cardinal girl knew. She had heard the maid singing while she worked.

After a while, Dr. Blackbird announced that he must leave. "Others want my help too," he told the cardinals. Really, he was worried that the cardinals would find out about the missed lessons. Then they might ask for their money back. So Dr. Blackbird flew away.

The same day, the rich cardinal decided that his daughter should give a recital. All of the neighbor birds would come. "You can show us what you learned from Dr. Blackbird," he said. And a day for the recital was set.

The cardinal girl was thrown into a panic. "What will I do?" she cried, once alone. "I can't sing in front of all the other birds! I'll make a fool of myself! And Father will find out how little I practiced and learned from the teacher. He is going to be very disappointed." And she began to sob.

Just then she heard her maid singing in the hall. It was just soft singing, but very beautiful. The cardinal girl got an idea. She wiped her eyes and flew to the maid's side.

"Help me," she begged. "Your voice is so beautiful. And mine is just plain. You practiced what the teacher taught. I did not. Now I have to give a recital, and I'm going to make a fool of myself. You must help me."

"How can I help you?" asked the mockingbird.

"Come with me," said the cardinal girl. "We must go to see the village carpenter. On the way, I will tell you my idea."

The village carpenter was a woodpecker. He was happy to help out for a small fee. And so, during the days before the recital he worked in secret. He tap-tap-tapped a hole in the trunk of a great tree. He tapped until the hole was just the right size for a mockingbird.

On the recital day, the mocking-bird hid inside the hole in the tree. The cardinal girl stood in front of her. She perched on the edge of the hole. When the cardinal opened her beak to sing, all the birds were amazed. They had never heard such sweet singing before. Such a variety of notes and tunes! They clapped and whistled and cheered. Of course, they thought they were clapping for the cardinal girl. Little did they know that the mockingbird was really the one singing. The cardinal was only pretending to sing. (She was, as we say, lip-synching. Or, really, she was beak-synching. After all, birds don't have lips.)

   The Mockingbird's First Recital

Song after song brought more clapping and cheering from the amazed crowd. Only the cardinal father did not clap and cheer. He frowned. His daughter was not just better than she had been a few months ago. She was *so* much better that he could not believe it. Something fishy *must* be going on.

"That's enough singing," said the cardinal father, all of a sudden. "It's time to greet your fans, Daughter. Come down from that perch."

But the cardinal girl could not come down. She could not step away from her place in front of the hole. If she did, everyone would see the mockingbird behind her.

The father grew impatient. "Come down this instant!" he ordered. And at last his daughter obeyed. She fluttered to the ground looking miserable. The mockingbird now could be seen by one and all. The crowd began to murmur and point.

"Step forward, Miss," said the rich cardinal to the mockingbird.

The young maid shyly stepped out of the shadows.

"Here, I believe," said the cardinal father, "is the real star of the show we have just seen. I wanted my daughter to be a star," he told the crowd. "But it seems to me this young bird is the one destined to be famous. Perhaps she will share another song with us now."

"Yes! Yes! Encore!" cried all the birds in the crowd, clapping.

And from that day until this, the mockingbird and all of her children and grandchildren have been famous for their singing.

MOCKINGBIRDS

- Mockingbirds are medium-sized gray birds. They have a stripe of white on each wing. This white stripe is easy to see when they spread their wings.
- Mockingbirds copy the songs of other birds. They have been known to copy many other sounds as well. They can sound just like creaking fences, dogs' barking, car alarms, and cell phone rings! They can copy human words, too.
- Mockingbirds were popular pets in the 1800s. People stole baby mockingbirds from nests. So many babies were trapped that wild mockingbirds became rare in some places. (They're not rare now.) Pet buyers paid big bucks to get the best singers. Some mockingbirds sold for 50 dollars and more. That was a *huge* amount of money at the time!
- You won't see mockingbirds at your bird feeder. That's because they don't eat seeds. Mockingbirds like to eat insects and fruit.
- Mockingbirds are tough! And once they've picked out their home turf, everybody else had better clear out! Mockingbirds will dive-bomb dogs, cats, and even people. They chase other birds out of their yard. Sometimes mockingbirds also trick other birds into leaving. They do it by copying a sound that's scary to other birds, such as a hawk's call.
- The mockingbird is the state bird of five U.S. states: Arkansas, Florida, Mississippi, Tennessee, and Texas.

Be a Backyard Birder

The best way to find a mockingbird is by listening. But chances are you'll be able to spot the bird that's doing that crazy singing! Mockingbirds like to sit in places where they can be seen singing.

EXTENSION ACTIVITY: SONG RECORDERS

Concepts: observing the natural world, making a record of observations, developing listening skills

For this activity, you will need:

a tape recorder or digital recorder

pencils

paper

- If you live in an area where mockingbirds are common, take the child or children to a yard or park.
- When you hear a mockingbird singing, have the child or children record the song. Some relatives of the northern mockingbird have a similar imitative singing style. The gray catbird is one such bird. If you hear a catbird rather than a mockingbird, you may record its song for this exercise.
- Once indoors again, pass out paper and pencils. Say: "Mockingbirds copy the songs of other birds and put them all together when they sing. Let's see how many different songs our mockingbird copied to make up his song."
- Play the recording, stopping it frequently. Have children write down each separate birdsong they can hear. Song translations might be written in phrases such as "cheep cheep chireep" or in whatever word-sounds children hear. Encourage children to be creative and humorous in their transcriptions.
- Have children listen for times when the mockingbird (catbird, etc.) is repeating a phrase he/she has already sung. Have children count up the number of separate songs they hear.

- Alternatively, take the child or children to an outdoor area where birdsong can be heard. Record any and all birds for a period of five minutes. Back indoors, replay the recording in a stop-and-start fashion. Have children make transcriptions of all the songs they hear, noting times an already transcribed song is being repeated.

Chapter 14

Owl

Appropriate for grades:

K-4

Reading level of story and fact file:

2.0

INTRODUCTION FOR PARENTS AND TEACHERS

Owls live on every continent except Antarctica. They have always been the subject of folktales and superstitions. Many cultures have viewed owls negatively, associating them with death, bad luck, and black magic (Tate 91–94). In ancient Greece, however, the owl was sacred to Athene, the goddess of war and wisdom (96–97). From this association is descended our modern-day figure of the wise old owl, found in the nursery rhyme and in children's stories ranging from A. A. Milne's *Winnie-the-Pooh* to Disney's *The Fox and the Hound.*

The folktale in this chapter is a pourquoi tale from Mexico. The Cu Bird of the story is a mythical bird. The story explains the origin of the owl's call and why owls only come out at night. The owl in this story is a wise old owl that leads the other birds. Another tale in this collection that contains a similar figure is "The King of All Birds," a folktale presented in the chapter on wrens. For variations on the story of "The Owl and the Cu Bird," see the Works Consulted list.

An award-winning picture book that you may also wish to share with children is Jane Yolen's *Owl Moon.* The story depicts a young girl and her father as they walk through the winter woods at night, looking for a Great Horned Owl.

101

Much of the information about owls in this chapter, including that presented in the **Feathered Facts File,** is taken from Cornell University's *All About Birds* Web site. You can visit this site at http://www.allaboutbirds.org/guide/Great_Horned_Owl/id to learn more about great horned owls and other owl species, find photographs of owls, and listen to recordings of their calls.

STORY SHARING STRATEGY

Cut out a bird shape or draw one on the board. This can be your Cu bird. Before reading the story to children, pass out feathers, one per child. The feathers should be of many colors. When you reach the point in the story where the birds agree to each loan the Cu bird a feather, prompt the children to decorate the Cu bird by sticking their feathers, one at a time, onto the bird shape. You may also wish to hide the decorated Cu bird from sight at the point in the story where the Cu bird flies off into the depths of the forest.

DISCUSSION OR WRITING PROMPT

Before reading the **Feathered Facts File** on owls, ask children, "What do you know about owls? What do you think of when you think of owls?" Have children free-associate about owls. List the children's ideas on the board, or have children take turns adding items to the list. Now read the chapter's fact file together. Then return to the list of owl associations. Have the children mark FACT next to anything listed that is scientifically true.

The Owl and the Cu Bird

A folktale from Mexico as told by Jennifer Kroll

Long ago, when the world was new, the birds did not yet have their feathers. Owl was the leader of birds. He sent a message out to all the other birds.

"It's time to come and choose your feathers," he said.

So all the birds came. They flew in from north and south and east and west. They chose feathers for themselves. Some birds chose feathers that were bright red or yellow or blue. Some chose feathers that were black or white or tan. Some birds chose feathers of several different colors. Pretty soon, all the feathers were gone.

But one bird was late in getting to the meeting. This was the Cu bird. By the time she got there, all the feathers had been taken.

"Oh dear me!" sighed the Cu bird. "The other birds have left no feathers for me. What will become of me? The night is cold and I have no feathers to keep me warm. The wind is strong, but I have no feathers to help me fly. Oh dear me." And she began to cry.

Owl felt sorry for the Cu bird. "It isn't right that the Cu bird should have no feathers," he said to the other birds. "We should share our feathers with her."

But the other birds did not want to share their feathers.

"We're happy with our feathers. We like how we look," they told Owl. "It's not our fault the Cu bird was so late in getting to the meeting. If she had been on time, she would have feathers, too."

Owl agreed that this was true. "But we still should share," he said. "The Cu bird has no feathers at all. And each of us can surely spare one feather. If we each give one, she will have enough feathers to cover her."

Many birds still didn't want to give a feather. But after awhile, they agreed to Owl's plan.

"Each of us will give Cu one feather," they said. "But we will only give the feathers on loan. Cu must agree to give back our feathers when she finds or grows some of her own."

"Very well," said Owl. "Give me your feathers and I will bring them to Cu."

"How can we be sure that she will return them when she's done with them?" the birds all wanted to know.

"I will make sure she returns your feathers," said Owl. "You have my word."

So each of the birds gave Owl a feather. And Owl took the feathers to the Cu bird.

Cu put the feathers on herself one at a time. She put on a red feather from the cardinal and a blue feather from the bluebird. She put on a yellow feather from the canary and a green feather from the parrot. She put on a white feather from the swan and a black feather from the crow. Soon she was covered in feathers of every color.

"Ooh! Look at me!" Cu said. She gazed at her own reflection in some water. "I'm the most beautiful bird in the world!"

"Yes," said Owl to the Cu bird. "You do look lovely. But remember—the feathers you are wearing are just on loan. You will have to give them back someday."

"I don't think I'll ever want to give these feathers back," said Cu. "But thank you just the same for all your help." And off she flew into the depths of the forest.

And to this day, Cu has never given those feathers back. She knows that she is in trouble with the other birds. So she seldom lets herself be seen. But perhaps someday you will spot her out of the corner of your eye. If you do, you will be dazzled by her feathers of every color. You will think to yourself: "I have just seen the most beautiful bird in all the world."

Yes, you may see the Cu if you are very lucky. But don't try looking for her. Chances are, you'll never find her that way. Owl has been looking for her all these years. He gave his word that he would get those feathers back. And so he

     The Owl and the Cu Bird

keeps looking and looking. But he never finds Cu. She is too good at hiding. Owl is too ashamed to show his face to other birds during the day. So he only comes out at night now. If you are out some night, you just might hear him. "Cu!" he calls as he searches for the lost Cu bird. "Cu! Cu! Cu!"

GREAT HORNED OWLS

- Great horned owls have big feather tufts above their ears. The tufts look like horns. That's how these owls got their name.
- Great horned owls can be up to two feet long. Their wings can be up to five feet wide when spread out for flying.
- These big birds live on the frozen Arctic tundra. They live in rainforest areas. They probably live in your neighborhood, too. They are one of the most common kinds of owls in North America.
- Great horned owls catch and eat mice, rabbits, weasels, squirrels, raccoons, and birds. Sometimes they even eat other meat-eating birds such as hawks.
- Skunks for lunch? Most predators say "no way" to such a stinky snack. But great horned owls have no sense of smell. They love to eat skunks.
- Most birds have one eye on each side of their heads. An owl's eyes both look forward, just like a person's eyes do. Great horned owls can see very well in the dark.
- Some people believe owls can turn their heads all the way around. That's not true. They can turn their heads much farther than we can, though. Owls have to turn their heads in order to look in a new direction. They can't move their eyes the way we can.
- A great horned owl has a much better sense of hearing than you do. Its hearing helps it find food. The fringes on the owl's wings help it stay very quiet as it swoops in on its next meal.

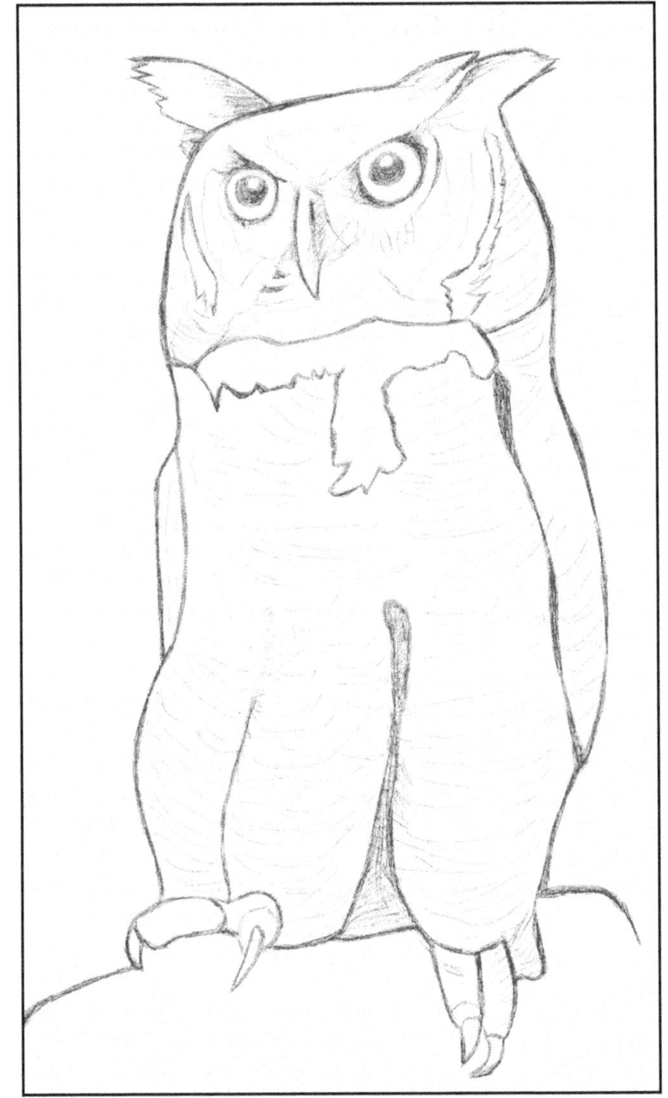

Be a Backyard Birder

Owls are mostly up and about when the world is dark. That means they're often easier to hear than to spot. Great Horned Owls usually hoot about three to eight times in a row. Some people think they sound like they're saying, "Who's awake? Me too."

EXTENSION ACTIVITY: FOOD CHAIN FLIP CARD GAME

Concepts: the food chain; also spelling and reading practice for younger children

For this activity, you will need:

blank index cards

pencil

pen or marker

- Print the names of animals and plants on 26 blank index cards. Print "plants or seeds" on eight cards. Print "rabbit" on four cards. Print "mouse" on four cards. Print "blackbird" on four cards. Print "red-tailed hawk" on four cards. Print "great horned owl" on two cards. (Or you may wish to have the children make the cards for the game.)
- Introduce the term *food chain* and talk about what a food chain is. Tell children that they are going to play a food chain game.
- Read the names of the animals on the cards aloud. Discuss the different plants and animals with the children. Talk about what each animal eats. The mouse and blackbird both eat seeds. The rabbit eats plants. These animals do not eat each other. The red-tailed hawk and great horned owl eat rabbits, blackbirds, and mice. The great horned owl also eats red-tailed hawks.
- Demonstrate how to play Food Chain Flip. The game is similar to War. The cards are shuffled and dealt out into two face-down piles. The two players flip the cards on top of their piles simultaneously. The player whose card says the name of the animal highest on the food chain wins the pair. If neither of the animals/plants flipped is higher on the food chain than the other, the players each take back their own cards. Players go on to flip the next pair, then the next. After all cards are flipped, players reshuffle their cards into facedown piles. The players then flip their piles again. Players can play a set number of rounds or until one player holds all the cards. The player with the most cards wins.
- Give children a chance to take turns playing the game.
- To extend the activity, have children research other food chains and create food chain flip card decks based on what they learn. You might wish to assign each child a different geographic area or habitat zone to research. For example, one child might be assigned to create a Brazilian rainforest food chain deck. Another child might be assigned to create an Atlantic Ocean food chain deck. A third child might be assigned to create an Arctic tundra food chain deck. And so forth. Children may make wish to make their card decks more elaborate by adding pictures of the animals and plants to the cards.

Chapter 15
Robin

Appropriate for grades:

K-4

Reading level of story and fact file:

2.6

INTRODUCTION FOR PARENTS AND TEACHERS

The tale contained in this chapter was told in Ireland and parts of Europe and is also remarkably similar to a tale told by the Sechelt Nation of British Columbia. In the Irish/European version of the tale, the sleeping baby saved by the robin is often (though not always) said to have been the Baby Jesus. Sometimes the events of the story are said to have taken place on Christmas Eve, and sometimes they are said to have happened during the flight of the Holy Family into Egypt.

Other tales of how the robin got its red breast told by North American peoples such as the Mewuk, Yokut, and Micmac (see Works Consulted), as well as by Europeans from the Isle of Guernsey (Tate 124), also have overlapping themes. In these cases the robin is similarly singed by fire while carrying out a good deed. The robin is the bringer of fire to humans or the bringer of sun to the dark world. It is interesting to note how positive characteristics such as helpfulness, cheerfulness, and piousness almost always seem to be attributed to the robin in folklore (Tate 118–22).

The facts presented in this chapter's **Feathered Facts File** pertain to the American robin. The European robin is a separate species. Much of the information about robins in this chapter, including that presented in the **Feathered Facts File,** is taken from Cornell

University's *All About Birds* Web site. You can visit this site at http://www.allaboutbirds.org/guide/American_Robin/id to learn about the life history of robins, find photographs of these birds, and listen to recordings of their songs and calls.

STORY SHARING STRATEGY

Children may enjoy acting out this folktale. Have students read the story silently, or read it aloud together once. Then assign parts to the children. You will need a father, mother, grandfather, baby, robin, and several scary/dangerous wild animals. Designate a spot in the room that will be the campsite. Encourage the children to be creative in finding/developing other props such as materials that can be built up into a pretend fire. Older children who are very familiar with plays can be encouraged to rewrite the story as a play script and then act it out.

DISCUSSION OR WRITING PROMPT

Say: This story is about an animal that helps to save a baby. It is just a story. But have you ever heard of any real animals that have saved people's lives? Do you think animals can be heroes?

How the Robin Got Its Red Breast

An Irish folktale as told by Jennifer Kroll

Long ago, a father, a mother, and a grandfather were traveling with a baby. This was a time before cars, or roads, or hotels. The family had to go on foot. They were far from any village when they stopped for the night. The father built a roaring fire.

"I fear the wild creatures in these woods," said the mother. "I hear the wolves howling not so far away. And from time to time I see the glow of eyes in the brush. I fear some hungry animal has its eye on our baby."

"If we stay near the fire and keep it going, we will all be safe," said the father. "The wild creatures will not go near the flames." He fed the fire another piece of wood. The flames leapt up. "You should get some rest now," he said to the mother and grandfather. "You must be very tired from our travels. Sleep, and I will tend the fire."

"Wake me when you grow weary. Then I will take my turn," said the mother to her husband.

"And I must have my turn as watchman, too," said the grandfather. "We will all have a turn."

"Yes," agreed the father. "That way, we can all get some rest."

The baby was already sleeping. Soon the mother and grandfather slept, too. Only the father was awake. He fed the fire and fanned the coals. He listened to the cricket's song. He heard the distant howl of the wolves.

But after some hours, his eyelids began to droop. "I can stay awake no longer," he said to himself. And he woke the mother gently.

"I guess it's my turn," she said drowsily. And she sat up and took her place beside the fire.

For hours, the mother kept watch. She listened to the hoot of an owl. She saw the glow of animal eyes in the dark. She fed the fire another piece of wood. Then, after some time, her eyelids also began to droop.

"I can stay awake no longer," she said to herself. And she wakened the grandfather.

"I will care for the fire until morning light," said the grandfather. "Rest now, my dear."

So the mother went to sleep. And grandfather sat up and tended the fire.

But after a bit, his eyelids too began to droop. The grandfather pinched himself and poked himself. He tried to stay awake. But it was no use. Before long, he was fast asleep.

And while he slept, the fire burned down. Down and down it burned to almost nothing. Finally, all that was left was one glowing coal. Hungry wild animals crept in closer. They had been afraid of the fire. But now, the sleeping baby looked like easy prey.

Luckily, the family was not alone. A robin lived in a nearby  tree. She usually slept until dawn. But she had wakened early. And now she saw that the human baby was in danger. Quickly, the robin swooped down to the campfire. With her wings spread, she fanned the glowing coal. A flame leapt from the coal. For hours, the robin worked to keep that little fire burning. Flames scorched the gray bird. But she did not give up. Only when the human father wakened in the early dawn did the bird fly off. The father saw the bird's breast as she flew. It was red from the flames.

And so the robin's breast has been—from that day to this.

     How the Robin Got Its Red Breast

ROBINS

- Robins are gray birds with red tummies. Males and females look just a bit different. Males have darker tummies and have blacker heads. Young robins have speckles on their tummies.

- Robins don't eat seeds. So you won't find them at your birdfeeder. Robins like to eat worms. They also eat insects and fruit. They eat mostly berries in the wintertime.

- It's funny to watch a robin hunting for worms. The robin will make several hops across the ground. Then it will tilt its head to one side. The bird looks like it's listening for worms. But really the robin is looking for signs of dirt moving.

- Robins' eggs are about the size of a quarter. They are a beautiful blue color. Mother robins lay three to five eggs at a time. They sit on their eggs for about two weeks. Fathers take a turn once in a while, too.

- The robin is the state bird of Connecticut, Michigan, and Wisconsin.

- Robins live year 'round in most U.S. states. They join up into big groups in winter. These groups can have thousands of birds in them!

- Some animals eat robins' eggs and young. But people are the biggest killer of adult robins. People put poisons on lawns to kill bugs and weeds. Robins hunt for food on lawns. So robins get poisoned right along with the bugs and weeds.

Be a Backyard Birder

Some people say that a robin's song sounds like, "Cheer up! Cheer up! Cheerily!" Robins also make a "Yeep! Cluck-cluck-cluck!" call when they sense danger. Look and listen for robins at the park or on your way to school. What are the robins around your neighborhood saying today?

EXTENSION ACTIVITY: ROBIN AND WORM WATCH!

Concepts: observing nature, charting observations, using a calendar, measuring temperature

For this activity, you will need:

a calendar

a thermometer

a shovel and bucket (optional)

- This activity is intended for use in areas where winter temperatures get below freezing. In late winter, share this chapter's folktale and feathered facts with the children. Talk about how a robin on the lawn is often thought of as a sign of spring. In most parts of the United States, robins are actually year-'round residents. But they become much more noticeable in the spring. Then, all of a sudden, robins can be seen hopping around on lawns.

- Ask children why they think this is the case. Have the children recall what they have learned about robins' feeding habits. What are robins' favorite foods and why does the temperature need to be above freezing for robins to eat one of their favorite foods? Share the fact that worms migrate deeper into the soil when the temperature gets below freezing. They come back to the surface when it warms up.

- Tell the children that you are all going to watch for spring by watching for robins hunting worms. Have children point out or report when they see a robin hopping around on the ground. Have children also check the temperature on such days. You may wish to have children mark their robin sightings and the daily temperature on a calendar. Ask children to decide: How warm does it need to be in order for robins to hunt for worms?

- As part of this activity, you may also wish to sample the soil. When robins have been sighted on the ground a number of times, take a large shovelful of dirt and place it in a bucket.

- Encourage children to dig through the dirt looking for worms.

Chapter 16

Sparrow

Appropriate for grades:

K-4

Reading level of story and fact file:

3.1

INTRODUCTION FOR PARENTS AND TEACHERS

Sparrows live almost everywhere. Over 50 varieties exist in the United States and Canada. Each has a slightly different look. The sparrow pictured and described in the **Feathered Facts File** is the song sparrow. It is one of the most common types of North American sparrows. But you may wish to introduce students to other local sparrow species, too.

The story in this chapter is based on a Japanese folktale. The Monkey Dance and Sparrow Dance are Japanese folk dances. This pourquoi tale explains the origin of the two folk dances and of general differences in men's and women's dance styles.

Much of the information about sparrows in this chapter, including that presented in the **Feathered Facts File,** is taken from Cornell University's *All About Birds* Web site. You can visit this site at http://www.allaboutbirds.org/guide/Song_Sparrow/id to learn about song sparrows and other sparrow species, see photographs of these birds, and listen to recordings of their songs and calls.

115

STORY SHARING STRATEGY

Before reading the story, tell children that this story is about dancing sparrows and dancing monkeys. Have the children pretend to be dancing sparrows. How do the children think sparrows would dance? Why?

Next, have the children pretend to be dancing monkeys. How do the children think monkeys would dance? Why?

You may wish to divide the group of children into monkeys and sparrows. Seat monkeys and sparrows separately. Tell children that you are going to read the story. During the story they will get a chance to do their monkey and sparrow dances again. Cue sparrows and monkeys to do their dances when the animals dance in the story.

DISCUSSION OR WRITING PROMPT

Ask children: Have you ever gone for a walk in the woods? What animals did you see? What were they doing? Tell children: In this story, a man and woman walk into the woods and come upon animals dancing and having parties. Have children write stories in which they walk into the woods and see animals doing something surprising.

The Dancing Monkeys and the Dancing Sparrows

A folktale from Japan as told by Jennifer Kroll

An old man and his wife lived in a little house near the forest. One day, the old man went into the forest to cut firewood. He took a turn down an unfamiliar path. As he walked he began to hear the sound of music and drums. Somewhere, deep in the forest, someone was playing a lively dance tune. The old man wondered who it could be. He kept walking and the music got louder. The old man came around a bend. And what he saw astonished him. There, in a clearing of

the forest, a group of monkeys seemed to be having a party. Some of the monkeys were keeping time on drums while others played little horns. Some monkeys were dancing wildly, leaping and chattering. Still others were passing around little bottles made from gourds. The monkeys all seemed to be having a wonderful time. The old man wished at once that he could join their party.

"Hello!" he cried, stepping out from behind a tree, into the clearing.

At once the music stopped. The dancing monkeys stopped dancing. The monkeys all turned and looked at the old man. They looked just for a second. And then they all let out cries of alarm. Away the monkeys scampered, as fast as they could go. Up into the trees they scurried and out of sight. In a moment's time, the clearing was completely empty.

The old man stared at the place where the monkeys had been. For a moment, he wondered if he had imagined the whole thing. After all, who ever heard of dancing monkeys? What a crazy thing to dream up! But then, the old man noticed something. Lying on the ground was one of the little gourd bottles. In their hurry to get away, the monkeys had left it behind.

The old man picked up the gourd bottle. It had a stopper in the top of it. He pulled out the stopper and smelled the drink inside. The stuff in the bottle didn't smell like anything he'd ever had to drink before. But it did smell fruity and delicious. The old man decided to bring the drinking gourd home with him. That way, he would have something to show his wife. Maybe she would believe his crazy story if she saw the drinking gourd and smelled the drink inside. The old man put the stopper back into the gourd bottle. He carried the bottle home with him.

Little did the old man know, but something strange was also happening to his wife. She was walking down to the river with a load of laundry. As she walked, the old woman could hear the sound of many birds singing. This might not have caught her attention. But the birdsong was quite unusual. It sounded to the woman as if the birds all were singing the same song. And the song they sang was lovely. It was a lilting, pretty tune that almost made the old woman feel like dancing. (And she had not done that in many years.) The old woman wanted to see what birds were making this wonderful song. She set down her laundry at the edge of the path and walked a little way into the forest.

She had not gone far when she spotted the birds. The singing birds were sparrows. They were perched in the branches of a great tree. Beneath the tree were even more sparrows. Some of them were passing around little gourd bottles filled with something to drink. Others were dancing a graceful dance. The sparrows hopped and stepped and fluttered together over the ground. The

   The Dancing Monkeys and the Dancing Sparrows

old woman admired their dance. She wanted to get an even closer look. She quietly took one step forward, then another.

Crack! The old woman had stepped on some twigs. At once the singing and dancing stopped. The sparrows all turned and looked at the old woman. They looked just for a moment. Then one of them let out a call of alarm. Away the sparrows all flew together. In a heartbeat, every last sparrow was out of sight.

The old woman stared at the place where the sparrows had been. For a moment, she wondered if she had imagined the whole thing. After all, who ever heard of dancing sparrows? What a crazy thing to dream up! But then, the old woman noticed something. Lying on the ground was one of the little gourd bottles. In their hurry to get away, the sparrows had left it behind.

The old woman picked up the gourd bottle. She pulled out its stopper and smelled the drink inside. The stuff in the bottle didn't smell like anything she'd ever had to drink before. But it did smell flowery and delicious. The old woman decided to bring the drinking bottle home to show her husband. Perhaps, she thought, if he saw the bottle he might believe her strange story.

"You'll never believe what I saw today," the old man later told his wife.

"And you'll *really* never believe what I saw today," the old woman said to her husband.

Then they told each other the stories of what they had seen in the woods. They were amazed to find their tales so much alike.

"I kept one of the bottles and brought it back to show you," said the husband.

"I kept one of the bottles, too," said the wife.

They laughed and exchanged the little gourd bottles.

The wife smelled the drink inside the monkey gourd. "Mmmm. This smells delicious!" she said. "I think I'll try a little sip." And she did.

The husband smelled the drink inside the sparrow gourd. "I wonder what this stuff is," he said. "It sure smells good. I think I'll try some, too." And he did.

And then, the old man and the old woman felt something strange happening to them. They had been feeling rather tired after their day of walking and work. But now they didn't feel tired at all. Instead, they felt like dancing. In fact, they could hardly stop their feet from moving. The old man and old woman both got up and began to dance. They started to sing, as well. Then they began to laugh and leap and made lots of noise. And soon the neighbors came over to see what was happening. It was a funny sight to see! What was funniest of all was the way the man and woman were dancing. You see, the old woman was leaping around like a monkey as she danced. She had taken a drink from the monkey gourd. The old man fluttered and hopped and took little graceful steps. He was dancing like a sparrow because he had taken a drink from the sparrow gourd.

"What's going on?" the neighbors wanted to know.

And the old man and the old woman told their story. But they hardly paused to tell it. Their feet wanted to keep dancing so badly.

"You look funny!" one of the neighbors said. "You look like you're dancing the wrong dances."

"Yes," another neighbor agreed. "Maybe you should each try drinking from the other bottle."

So they did. The old man took a drink from the monkey gourd. And instead of dancing like a graceful sparrow, he began to leap like a monkey. The old woman took a drink from the sparrow gourd. And instead of leaping like a monkey, she began to do a pretty bird dance.

Then the old man and woman gave drinks to their neighbors, too. All the women and girls took drinks from the sparrow bottle. And all the men and boys took drinks from the monkey bottle. And they all began to dance like monkeys and sparrows.

And to this day, men and boys still tend to look like monkeys when they dance. And women and girls still tend to look like sparrows. And if you don't believe that's true, look around sometime when you're in a room full of dancing people. You'll see monkeys and sparrows everywhere.

  The Dancing Monkeys and the Dancing Sparrows

SONG SPARROWS

- Do you live in the desert? In the mountains? By the ocean? In a city? People live in many different kinds of places. And song sparrows do, too. Song sparrows live in almost every part of the U.S. and Canada.
- Song sparrows are streaked brown and gray. Their tummies are lighter colored than their wings and heads. They are about four and a half to six and a half inches long.
- Song sparrows may look pretty ordinary. But, boy, can they sing! Male song sparrows sometimes have singing contests. The birds take turns showing off their singing skills. They try to impress a female.
- Song sparrow pairs hunt together for a good nest spot. They often build their nests on the ground or at the base of a bush. These birds often use the same nest spots over and over.
- Berries and seeds are what they eat. Song sparrows also eat insects.
- The song sparrow is just one kind of sparrow. About 50 kinds of sparrows live in North and South America.

Be a Backyard Birder

Birds need water, as well as food. Some people put out special birdbaths. But a pan of clean water will work as a birdbath, too. Make sure to take ice off the birdbath in freezing winter weather. Add warm water. The birds will thank you!

EXTENSION ACTIVITY: MAKING A PINECONE BIRD FEEDER

Concepts: animal eating habits; the life cycle of conifers

For this activity, you will need:

Pinecones (at least one large one for each child present)

Peanut butter or vegetable shortening

Butter knife or knives

Bag of birdseed

One or more dishes or bowls

String or twine

Decorative ribbon (optional)

- Set up as you would for an art activity. Set supplies out. Pass out one or more pinecones to each child present.
- Have children look at and talk about the pinecones before undertaking the project. Ask children what kind of trees produce pinecones. Ask why the trees produce the cones. Point out that the cones they are looking at once contained seeds. These cones opened up and their seeds fell out. If possible, for contrast, show children a closed cone that has not yet lost its seeds.
- You may also wish to present children with edible pine nuts. You can purchase these at most grocery stores. Tell children that many kinds of birds eat the seeds that come out of pinecones. These seeds are sometimes called pine nuts. (You may wish to allow children to sample the pine nuts. But be aware that pine nut allergy is very serious and not uncommon.)
- Tell children that they are going to make bird feeders out of these old pinecones. Demonstrate the activity.
- Using a butter knife, put peanut butter or vegetable shortening on the various surfaces of the pinecone.
- Sprinkle seeds on the cone. Fill a bowl with birdseed and roll the pinecone in the bowl.
- Tie a string or ribbon around a pinecone so that it can be hung.
- Optionally, you may wish to have children add colorful bows to their feeders. A more complex, mobile-like feeder can be created by stringing multiple pinecones together.
- Hang up the feeders outdoors or send them home with children.

Chapter 17
Swallow

Appropriate for grades:

1–6

Reading level of story and fact file:

3.1

INTRODUCTION FOR PARENTS AND TEACHERS

Barn swallows are nearby neighbors to many of us in North America. Children may enjoy learning to identify these acrobatic, bug-eating birds. Barn swallows migrate, and often return to the very same place where they've previously nested. They have long been viewed in many parts of Europe as harbingers of spring (Tate 133–36). Children living near barn swallow colonies can be encouraged to watch for the arrival of the swallows in the spring and their disappearance in the fall. Children can visit Annenberg Media's *Journey North* Web site at http://www.learner.org/jnorth/swallow/index.html to find out when barn swallows have appeared locally and to record their own first spring sightings online.

Much of the information about swallows in this chapter, including that presented in the **Feathered Facts File,** is taken from Cornell University's *All About Birds* Web site. You can visit this site at http://www.allaboutbirds.org/guide/Barn_Swallow/id to learn more about the life history of barn swallows, see photographs of these birds, and listen to recordings of their songs and calls. An easy-reading picture book that you also may wish to share with children is *The Journey of a Swallow* by Carolyn Scrace (Franklin Watts, 1999). The book contains a map that shows swallow migration routes. *Song of the Swallows*, a 1948 Caldecott Award-winning picture book by Leo Politi, is also strongly recommended.

This chapter's tale, "The Happy Prince," is a classic story by the famous English author Oscar Wilde. In Wilde's tale, as in most folklore, the swallow is viewed as a virtuous bird. Wilde's is primarily a secular story, dealing with issues of poverty, class, and social injustice. However, the final passage of the story refers to God and angels. The story may therefore not be suitable for use in all classrooms. The story references the fact that swallows migrate and cannot survive in cold climates in winter.

STORY SHARING STRATEGY

Tell the children that in this story they will see things from the point of view of a statue that's up high on a pillar. Do you have a statue in your city or town (or school) with which children are familiar? If not, have children think of the Statue of Liberty or another very famous statue. (You may wish to present the children with a picture.) Ask them to close their eyes and imagine they are the famous statue. What do they see? What do they spend the day thinking about?

DISCUSSION OR WRITING PROMPT

Ask: What could the Happy Prince see when he was in his walled garden? How did he feel then? What could he see on top of the pillar? How did that make him feel?

Ask: Do you ever see things happening that make you feel sad, things you wish you could change? When and where do you see them (i.e., on TV? In your own neighborhood? While riding across town? etc.)?

The Happy Prince

Abridged and adapted from the classic tale by Oscar Wilde

High above the city, on a tall column, stood the statue of the Happy Prince. He was covered all over with thin leaves of fine gold. For eyes he had two bright sapphires. He was very much admired by everyone who looked up at him.

One night there flew over the statue a little swallow. His friends had gone away to Egypt six weeks before. Now he was on his way, too. But he needed to stop for the night. "I will stay there," he cried. And he landed just between the feet of the Happy Prince. "I have a golden bedroom," he said happily. And he prepared to go to sleep. But just as he was putting his head under his wing a large drop of water fell on him. "What a strange thing!" he cried. "There is not a single cloud in the sky. And yet it is raining. The climate in the north of Europe is really dreadful."

Then another drop fell.

"What is the use of a statue if it cannot keep the rain off?" he said. And he was about to fly away.

But before he had opened his wings, a third drop fell, so he looked up, and saw—Ah! What did he see?

The eyes of the Happy Prince were filled with tears, and tears were running down his golden cheeks. His face was so beautiful in the moonlight that the little swallow was filled with pity.

"Who are you?" he said.

"I am the Happy Prince."

"Why are you weeping then?" asked the swallow. "You have drenched me."

"When I was alive and had a human heart," answered the statue, "I did not know what tears were. I lived in the palace. In the daytime, I played with my friends in the garden. And in the evening I led the dance in the Great Hall. A high wall rose around the garden. But I never cared to ask what lay beyond it. Everything around me was so beautiful. My courtiers called me the Happy Prince. And happy I was, if pleasure is happiness. So I lived, and so I died. And now that I am dead they have set me up here so high that I can see all the ugliness and all the misery of my city. And though my heart is made of lead, yet I cannot help but weep."

"What? Is he not solid gold?" asked the swallow to himself. But he was too polite to ask it out loud.

"Far away," continued the statue, "in a little street there is a poor house. One of the windows is open. Through it, I can see a woman seated at a table. Her face is thin and worn. She has rough, red hands, all pricked by the needle, for she is a seamstress. She is embroidering flowers on a satin gown. The gown is for the loveliest of the queen's maids-of-honor to wear at the next court ball. In a bed in the corner of the room the woman's little boy is lying ill. He has a fever, and is asking for oranges. His mother has nothing to give him but river water, so he is crying. Swallow, swallow, little swallow, will you pluck out one of my eyes and bring it to her?"

"My friends are waiting for me in Egypt," said the swallow. "They are flying up and down the Nile River. Soon they will go to sleep in the tomb of the great king."

"Swallow, swallow, little swallow," said the Prince. "Won't you stay with me for one night, and be my messenger? The boy is so thirsty and his mother unhappy."

The Happy Prince looked so sad that the little swallow agreed. "It is very cold here," he said. "But I will stay with you for one night, and be your messenger."

"Thank you, little swallow," said the Prince.

So the swallow picked out a sapphire from one of the prince's eyes, and flew away with it in his beak over the roofs of the town.

He passed by the cathedral tower. He passed by the palace and heard the sound of dancing. A beautiful girl came out on the balcony with her boyfriend. "I hope my dress will be ready in time for the ball," she said. "I have ordered flowers to be embroidered on it. But the seamstresses are so lazy." He passed over the river, and saw the lanterns hanging on the masts of the ships. He passed over the ghetto.

At last he came to the poor house and looked in. The boy was tossing feverishly on his bed, and the mother had fallen asleep, she was so tired. In he hopped, and laid the great sapphire on the table beside the woman's thimble. Then he flew gently around the bed, fanning the boy's forehead with his wings. "How cool I feel," said the boy. "I must be getting better." And he sank into a refreshing sleep.

Then the swallow flew back to the Happy Prince, and told him what he had done. "It is strange," he remarked. "But I feel quite warm now, although it is so cold."

"That is because you have done a good action," said the Prince. And the little swallow began to think, and then he fell asleep. Thinking always made him sleepy.

The next day the swallow flew down to the harbor. He sat on the mast of a large vessel and watched the sailors hauling big chests out of the hold with ropes. "I am going to Egypt!" cried the swallow, but nobody listened. And when the moon rose he flew back to the Happy Prince.

"I have come to bid you good-bye," he cried.

"Swallow, swallow, little swallow," said the Prince. "Will you not stay with me one night longer?"

"It is winter," answered the swallow. "And the chill snow will soon be here. In Egypt the sun is warm on the green palm trees, and the crocodiles lie in the mud and look lazily around. Dear Prince, I must leave you, but I will never forget you. And next spring I will bring you back a beautiful jewel in place of the one you have given away."

"In the square below," said the Happy Prince, "there stands a little girl who sells matches all day. She has let her matches fall in the gutter. They are all spoiled. Her father will beat her if she does not bring home some money, and she is crying. She has no shoes or stockings, and her little head is bare. Pluck out my other eye and give it to her, and her father will not beat her."

"I cannot pluck out your other eye. You would be quite blind then," said the swallow.

"Swallow, swallow, little swallow," said the Prince. "Do as I command you."

So the swallow plucked out the Prince's other eye, and darted down with it. He swooped past the match girl, and slipped the jewel into the palm of her hand. "What a lovely bit of glass," cried the little girl. And she ran home, laughing.

Then the swallow came back to the Prince. "You are blind now," he said, "so I must stay with you."

All the next day the swallow sat on the Prince's shoulder, and told him stories of what he had seen in strange lands. He told him of the red ibises who stand in long rows on the banks of the Nile and catch goldfish in their beaks. He told him of the sphinx, who is as old as the world itself and lives in the desert. He told him of the merchants who walk slowly by the side of their camels.

"Dear little swallow," said the Prince. "You tell me of marvelous things. But more marvelous than anything is the suffering of men and of women. There is no mystery so great as misery. Fly over my city, little swallow, and tell me what you see there."

So the swallow flew over the great city. He saw the rich making merry in their beautiful houses, while the beggars were sitting at the gates. He flew into dark lanes. There he saw the white faces of starving children looking out at the black streets. Under the archway of a bridge two little boys were lying together, trying to keep warm. "How hungry we are!" they said. "You must not lie here," shouted the watchman. And they wandered out into the rain.

Then the swallow flew back and told the Prince what he had seen.

"I am covered with fine gold," said the Prince. "You must take it off, leaf by leaf, and give it to the poor of my city."

Leaf after leaf of the fine gold the swallow picked off, until the Happy Prince looked quite dull and gray. Leaf after leaf of the fine gold he brought to the poor. And the children's faces grew rosier. And they

laughed and played games in the street. "We have bread now!" they cried.

Then the snow came, and after the snow came the frost. The poor little swallow grew colder and colder, but he would not leave the Prince. He loved the Prince too much. He tried to keep himself warm by flapping his wings. But at last he knew that he was going to die. He had just strength to fly up to the Prince's shoulder once more. "Good-bye, dear Prince!" he murmured.

"I am glad that you are going to Egypt at last, little swallow," said the Prince. "You have stayed too long here."

"It is not to Egypt that I am going," said the Swallow. And he kissed the Happy Prince and fell down dead at his feet.

At that moment a curious crack sounded inside the statue. Its lead heart had snapped in two.

Early the next morning the Mayor was walking in the square below with the town councilors. As they passed the column he looked up at the statue. "Dear me! How shabby the Happy Prince looks!" the Mayor said. "His eyes are gone. He is golden no longer. And here is a dead bird at his feet! The Happy Prince is little better than a beggar! We must tear him down and put up a new statue."

          The Happy Prince

So they pulled down the statue of the Happy Prince. Then they melted it in a furnace. "What a strange thing!" said the overseer at the foundry. "This lead heart will not melt. We must throw it away." So they threw the Happy Prince's broken heart on a garbage heap where the dead Swallow was also lying.

"Bring me the two most precious things in the city," said God to one of his angels. And the angel brought him the lead heart and the dead bird.

"You have rightly chosen," said God. "For in the garden of Paradise this little bird shall sing for evermore. And in my city of gold the Happy Prince shall praise me."

BARN SWALLOWS

- Barn swallows are small birds with long forked tails. They are gray-blue on their backs and the tops of their wings. Their faces are reddish.

- Do flying bugs bug you? Then the barn swallow is your buddy. These birds eat flying insects for breakfast, lunch, and dinner. They catch insects and eat them in midair. Sometimes, barn swallows also swoop down and grab bugs off the surface of water.

- Barn swallows like living near people. They build their nests on walls, in rafters, and under bridges. They make their nests mostly from mud. They add in some hair, grass, and feathers. Both males and females work to build the nest.

- Barn swallows went west with the pioneers. Pioneers moving west cleared land and built houses and farms. In doing so, they made new homes for barn swallows. These birds were once mostly eastern birds. They now live throughout almost all of the U.S.—and much of Canada, too.

- Barn swallows are great acrobats! They are fun to watch as they swoop and dive. Barn swallows spend more time in the air than almost any other kind of bird.

- Barn swallows don't stop for baths. They just swoop down into the water and get themselves wet. Then they keep right on going.

Be a Backyard Birder

Want to visit some barn swallows? You can often find these fancy fliers near bridges. Watch them swoop out over the water to catch bugs.

EXTENSION ACTIVITY: TWO VIEWS

Concepts: observing the environment and recording observations; using observation tools such as magnifying glasses; comparing and contrasting

For this activity, you will need:

paper or student journal notebooks

pens or pencils

magnifying glasses or pocket microscopes (optional)

- Tell the children that you want them to practice looking at things from close up and from far away. Take the children to a park, yard, or garden. Have them spend some time in that environment, writing about what they see. Encourage them to look at things from close up. You may wish to supply children with magnifying glasses or pocket microscopes so that they can take an extra-close look.

- Then take children to a second locale. Select a high point such as a scenic viewpoint or an upper floor of a high building. Have children spend some time in that environment, writing about what they see—and don't see—from up high.

- Have children compare and contrast what they saw from the two locations. You may wish to make a Venn diagram, or have children create Venn diagrams, representing the similarities and differences in what could be seen from each of the two views.

- To conclude the activity, you may wish to discuss the fact that some scientists look at the world from close up (microbiologists, etc.), while others (astronomers, etc.) look at it from far away.

Chapter 18

Swan

Appropriate for grades:

K-4

Reading level of story and fact file:

2.5

INTRODUCTION FOR PARENTS AND TEACHERS

This chapter's tale, "The Wounded Swan," is a story from the Buddhist tradition. It details an episode from the Buddha's boyhood. In the story of the Buddha's life, Prince Siddhartha Gautama later gives up his wealth and royal position. Instead of becoming a king like his father, he chooses a life of poverty as an itinerant teacher and holy man.

Swans are native to most parts of the globe. Three types live in the wild in North America. The black-billed trumpeter swans and tundra swans are native species. However, the swans most of us probably see most often are not native to this part of the world. Orange-billed mute swans are an introduced species. They were brought over from Europe and Asia in order to decorate parks and gardens. Much of the information about swans in this chapter, including that presented in the **Feathered Facts File,** is taken from Cornell University's *All About Birds* Web site. You can visit this site at http://www.allaboutbirds.org to learn more about the various swan species, see photographs of these majestic birds, and listen to recordings of their calls.

Along with the story in this chapter, you may wish to introduce children to other famous swan stories such as Hans Christian Andersen's "The Ugly Duckling" and "The Wild Swans."

133

STORY SHARING STRATEGY

Use a felt board (flannelboard) as you tell the story. You will need the following figures: a king, a queen, a prince, a boy, an old man, and a swan. If you have the human figures but no swan, you can cut one out of white felt.

DISCUSSION OR WRITING PROMPT

Before sharing the story with students, ask them: "What do you think is the most precious thing in all of the world?" Have them share responses orally or write their responses in journals. Before beginning the story, tell the children that a wise man in the story is going to give his answer to this very question.

The Wounded Swan

A story from the Buddhist tradition, retold by Jennifer Kroll

Prince Siddhartha and his cousin Devadatta were out playing in the palace gardens. Devadatta had just gotten a new bow. He was showing off how well he could shoot. Some swans were flying overhead. Devadatta took aim.

"Watch this!" he said to Siddhartha. And he let an arrow fly.

Both of the boys saw the struck swan tumble out of the sky.

"Got it!" yelled Devadatta excitedly. He began to run toward the place where he thought the swan had fallen.

Prince Siddhartha ran too. He was the faster of the two boys and found the swan first. The swan had not been killed, but only injured. It was thrashing around in fear and pain. An arrow was sticking from its side.

Prince Siddhartha felt sorry for the creature. "Let me help you," he said, gently. He moved slowly toward the animal, speaking softly. He picked up the swan and held it close. Then he gently pulled the arrow from its side.

Nearby was a bush with special leaves. The Prince knew these leaves were sometimes used for medicine. He picked some of the leaves and pressed them against swan's wound. Then he started off for the palace, carrying the hurt swan in his arms.

Devadatta caught up with Prince Siddhartha. "What are you doing?" he asked, angrily. "That's my swan! Give it to me!"

But the Prince would not give his cousin the swan.

"I shot it, so it's mine!" said Devadatta. "I want to show it to everybody. I want the cook to serve it for supper tonight. Give it here!"

"I got to it first. So it's mine now," said Prince Siddhartha.

"Is not!"

"Is so!"

The boys argued all the way back to the palace. And there they took their argument before the king and queen.

"Please make Siddhartha give me the swan," Devadatta begged the king and queen. "I shot it and so it's mine."

"Please don't make me give him the swan," Siddhartha begged. "Devadatta wants to kill it. And I want to help it get well."

The king and queen were not sure what to do. They decided to call for the oldest, wisest person they knew. The wise man came to the palace.

"Please tell us which boy should get the swan," the king and queen said to the wise man. And they explained what had happened.

The wise man did not have to think long before giving an answer.

"The most precious thing in all the world is life itself," said the wise man. "And so I believe the swan belongs to the boy who wants to save its life."

"Thank you," said the king and queen. "That settles it. Prince Siddhartha shall have the swan."

Devadatta was angry. He pouted and sulked. He thought about ways to get even with his cousin later. But he had to go along with this decision.

So Prince Siddhartha kept the swan. He cared for it until its wound had healed. And when it was better, he set the swan free and watched it fly away.

          The Wounded Swan

SWANS

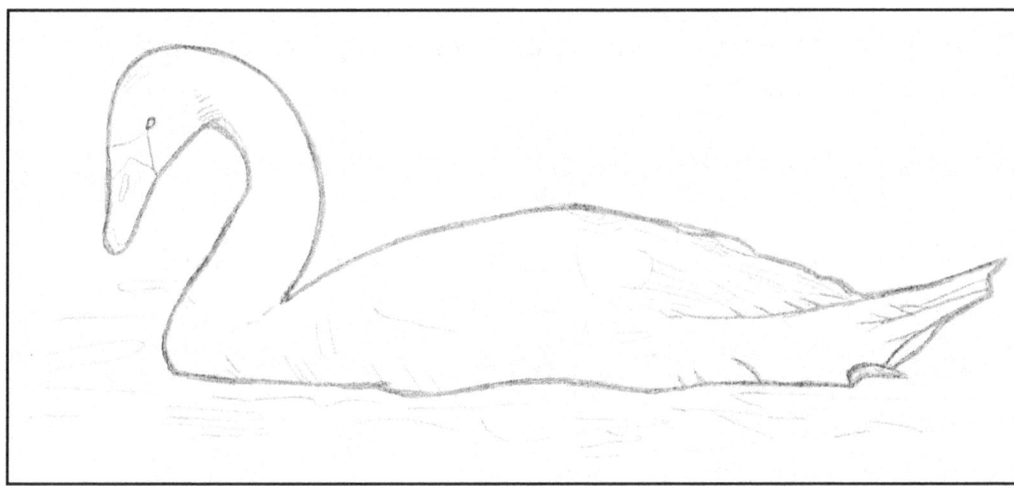

- Swans, ducks, and geese are sometimes called *waterfowl*. Swans are the largest type of waterfowl. Swans can weigh 25 to 35 pounds. Some swans have wings that are eight feet wide or more when spread out for flying.

- Swans are the largest type of birds that fly. Swans can fly at 50 to 60 miles an hour. That's as fast as a car on a highway. Some types of swans fly very long distances while migrating.

- Most types of swans are solid white. But not all. Black swans live in Australia and New Zealand. They are black all over. Black-necked swans live in South America. They have black heads and necks.

- Swans pair up with a mate at about three years of age. They usually stay with that mate for the rest of their lives.

- Swan babies are called cygnets.

- Trumpeter swans are large swans that are native to the U.S. and Canada. People once hunted so many of them that they almost became extinct. Their feathers were thought to make the best quill pens for writing.

Be a Backyard Birder

Swans often return to the same spot year after year. So once you spot them, you'll know where to keep looking! Don't get too close, though. Swans don't like having strangers too near their homes and babies. For a close-up look at swans, use binoculars.

EXTENSION ACTIVITY: WILD ANIMAL RESCUE ROLE PLAY

Concepts: animal characteristics and behavior; conducting research; presenting information through role play

For this activity, you will need:

access to research sources such as the Internet or a library

a chalkboard or whiteboard (optional)

chalk or dry-erase markers (optional)

poster board (optional)

markers or other art supplies (optional)

paper

pencils or pens

props for role play, possibly including stuffed animals

- In the story "The Wounded Swan," the young boy cares for an injured swan until it has healed. Many children are fascinated by the idea of wild animal rescue. The following research and role-play activity can help children learn more about wild animal rescue. Start by selecting an animal rescue scenario for the children to research and role-play. In a class situation, group or pair children and assign different scenarios to each group or pair. Scenarios might include finding a bird with an injured wing, finding a baby squirrel that has fallen from its nest, finding an injured rabbit, finding a litter of baby possums with a dead parent nearby, finding a bird tangled in fishing line, finding a seal covered in oil, and so forth.

- Prompt children to use the Internet or library to find out the best thing to do for the animal. Another way to find out may be to contact an authority such as a veterinarian, a wildlife center, or an organization such as the National Wildlife Rehabilitators' Association or the Audubon Society.

- Have children write down the steps that should be taken to help the animal. If these are to be shared with a class or group, they can be written on a chalkboard or whiteboard or printed on a poster or handout.

- Have children demonstrate what they have learned by acting out a scenario in which they find the animal in trouble and help it. Props can be used, including a stuffed animal (or a drawing of the animal), a cardboard box, a blanket, and whatever other materials may be appropriate.

- Encourage children to also share what should *not* be done and why. They may share this information orally and/or by demonstration.

Chapter 19

Turkey Vulture

Appropriate for grades:

2–6

Reading level of story and fact file:

2.7

INTRODUCTION FOR PARENTS AND TEACHERS

Turkey vultures are not among most people's favorite birds. Still, it is worth learning about and learning to identify these very common birds. Their soaring flight is fun to watch and, as scavengers, they play an important role in nature.

The folktale related in this chapter is a very common one that has been recorded many times over. It seems to have traveled from Nigeria to the United States, and has also been told in the Caribbean Islands and Brazil. Zora Neale Hurston, the African American writer and anthropologist most famous for her novel *Their Eyes Were Watching God*, recorded a version of it in her book *Mules and Men*, an exploration of African American folklore and folk culture in the American South. In the version that Hurston recorded, the vulture's (or buzzard's) repeated comment to the arrogant hawk is, "Ah waits on de salvation of de Lawd" (Hurston 117).

Much of the information about turkey vultures in this chapter, including that presented in the **Feathered Facts File,** is taken from Cornell University's *All About Birds* Web site. You can visit this site at http://www.allaboutbirds.org/guide/Turkey_Vulture/id to learn more about turkey vultures and see photographs of these birds.

STORY SHARING STRATEGY

Before or after reading. pass out strips of paper to the children. Tell the children to write a descriptive word on the strip of paper. The word should describe either the hawk or the vulture. Collect the strips of paper with descriptive words. Mix them and put in a bag or basket. Have each child draw out one of the descriptive words out and explain whether they think it describes the hawk or vulture and why.

DISCUSSION OR WRITING PROMPT

Say: The hawk tells the vulture, "If you want something, you have to go get it." Do you think that's true in life? Give examples from your own life of times when this has seemed to be true or untrue.

The Hawk and the Vulture

A folktale from Nigeria and the Southern United States as told by Jennifer Kroll

A hungry hawk was flying around, looking for something to eat. He saw a turkey vulture sitting in a tree. The vulture was just sitting there, doing nothing. The hawk dropped down onto a nearby branch.

"Good day, my friend," the hawk said to the turkey vulture. "What are you doing?"

"Oh, I'm just waiting for the world to turn," the turkey vulture said. And he didn't move a muscle.

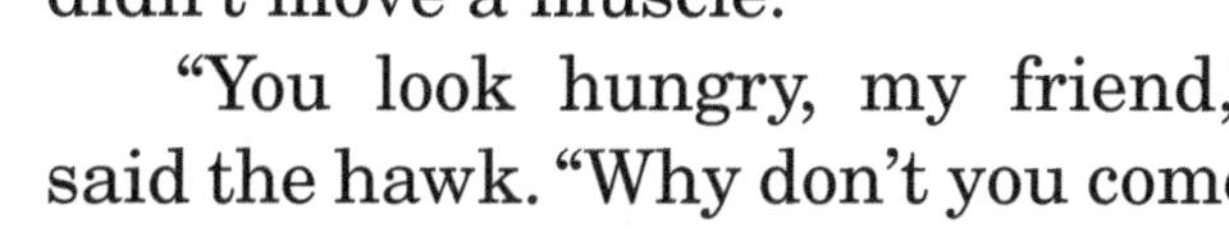

"You look hungry, my friend," said the hawk. "Why don't you come hunting with me? We'll catch a couple of mice or rabbits and make ourselves a nice lunch."

"No, thanks," said the turkey vulture. "I'm just waiting for the world to turn. When the world turns, I'll have my lunch."

The hawk couldn't believe the vulture's words. "You'll never get lunch this way," he laughed. "If you want something, you have to go get it. Don't you know that? Come on. Let's go hunt."

"Just go ahead without me," said the turkey vulture, without moving a muscle. "I have faith. I won't go hungry. When the world turns, I'll have my lunch."

"Foolish bird!" sneered the hawk. "But have it your own way. Sit here and starve. As for me, I'm going to take care of myself. I see a rabbit over there, running along that stone wall. He looks quite delicious. Off I go!" And the hawk zoomed off toward his prey.

The hawk wanted to show the vulture what a fine hunter he was. He wanted to laugh at the vulture while he enjoyed his lunch. But showing off is a dangerous business. The hawk dove too fast and ran head on into the stone wall. His lifeless body thumped down as the rabbit dashed out of sight.

"Ah," said the turkey vulture, looking down at the dead hawk. "Looks like it's lunch time." And with a few beats of his wide, fringed wings, he settled down for a good meal.

The Hawk and the Vulture

TURKEY VULTURES

- How is a turkey vulture like a turkey? In truth, they aren't much alike. But both types of birds do have featherless heads.
- Turkey vultures are really big birds! Their wingspan (the spread of their wings) can be about six feet.
- Turkey vultures aren't pretty birds— unless they're flying. These birds are very graceful in the air. They can soar for hours without flapping their wings. They ride on high currents of air called *thermals*.

- People sometimes mistake soaring turkey vultures for hawks or eagles. But turkey vultures are not close relatives of these hunting birds. Turkey vultures do not hunt. They have no sharp claws—or *talons*—on their feet.
- Turkey vultures eat mostly *carrion*. That's a fancy word for dead meat. They use their amazing sense of smell to find food. A turkey vulture flying above a thick forest can smell if there's something down there worth eating.
- Turkey vultures eat some plant foods, too. They are known to like pumpkins!
- A turkey vulture's eating habits might seem yucky to us. But these birds have an important job. They are part of nature's clean-up crew. They eat the bodies of animals that have died from diseases. This helps to stop the spread of disease.

Be a Backyard Birder

Turkey vultures fly higher than most other neighborhood birds. So look up! You will see them soaring in graceful loops above trees and fields.

EXTENSION ACTIVITY: T-REX AND TURKEY VULTURE VENN

Concepts: scavengers and their role in nature; comparing and contrasting; making and using a Venn diagram

For this activity, you will need:

a chalkboard or dry-erase board

chalk or markers

computer with Internet access (optional)

library access (optional)

- Read the story and **Feathered Facts File** with children. Or have children read these materials independently.
- Ask if children know what the term *scavenger* means. Explain the term and that turkey vultures are scavengers. Discuss the fact that scavengers play an important role in nature.
- Ask if children can think of any other scavengers besides turkey vultures. You may wish to have children conduct research online or at the library to identify other animals that are scavengers. Many kinds of hunting animals, such as hyenas, lions, foxes, and wolves, scavenge at times. Other animals that scavenge include raccoons, yellow jackets, opossums, and crows.
- Tell children that some scientists now believe that T-rex might have been mostly a scavenging animal. They believe this for several reasons. First, T-rex had very small arms. These arms would not have been very useful in catching prey. Secondly, T-rex seems to have had a really powerful sense of smell. Scientists can tell that by looking at T-rex fossil skulls. Animals that live by scavenging have to have a great sense of smell. Third, T-Rex had a heavy body and legs. It may not have been able to move fast enough to catch moving prey. Many scientists think T-rex could not even run. It could only walk fast.
- Optional: Present children with pictures of a turkey vulture and a T-rex or have the children locate pictures of these animals online and print out the pictures.
- Draw a Venn diagram of two overlapping ovals on the board—or make a poster on tagboard. Label one side T-rex and the other turkey vulture. Optional: Fasten pictures to the board in appropriate locations.
- Explain that the children will be making a Venn diagram to compare and contrast qualities of turkey vultures and T-rexes. Things that are true of both the T-rex and the turkey vulture will go in the overlapping portion of the diagram. Things that are true only of the T-rexes will go in the portion of the T-rex oval that does not overlap. Things true only of turkey vultures will go in the portion of the turkey vulture oval that does not overlap.
- Help the children to fill out the Venn diagram. Possible similarities might include: strong sense of smell, walks on two feet, cannot use feet to catch prey, eats carrion. You might add that both have/had three main toes on their feet. Differences should not be too difficult for children to point out.
- If you have been discussing/researching other scavenger animals with children, you may wish to extend the Venn diagram to include one or two additional animals.

Chapter 20
Woodpecker

Appropriate for grades:

K-6

Reading level of story and fact file:

3.0

INTRODUCTION FOR PARENTS AND TEACHERS

Woodpeckers can be seen and heard in almost any environment where trees and rotting wood are present. Their tap-tapping noises alert us to the fact that they're around. Once heard, many types of woodpeckers are also relatively easy to spot because their bodies are strikingly colored, with bold stripes or patches of red.

In folklore and mythology, woodpeckers are sometimes associated with thunder and lightning or with fire (Tate 149–50). The Romans associated these birds with agriculture and prophecy. And from ancient tales to Woody Woodpecker, these birds seem to have a reputation for being mischievous and naughty. A folktale recorded by novelist and anthropologist Zora Neale Hurston in her folklore collection *Mules and Men* tells how the woodpecker made holes in the floor of Noah's Ark and almost sunk it. His punishment for such troublesome activity was a blow to the head—an explanation for the red head that many types of woodpeckers have today (Hurston 103).

The Romanian folktale included in this chapter also associates woodpeckers with naughty behavior. It teaches a lesson about gossip and minding one's own business. Some versions of the story describe God, Jesus, or St. Peter turning an old woman into a woodpecker as punishment for letting her curiosity get the best of her (Tate 151–52, Lee 842).

145

Much of the information about woodpeckers in this chapter, including that presented in the **Feathered Facts File,** is taken from Cornell University's *All About Birds* Web site. You can visit this site at http://www.allaboutbirds.org/guide/search to learn about woodpecker species, see photographs of woodpeckers, and listen to recordings of their calls and drumming noises.

STORY SHARING STRATEGY

You may wish to give children the chance to act out this story. Supply the children with props such as an empty box, a magic wand, and capes. Or give children the task of designing and gathering their own props. Assign the roles of Mrs. Schmidt, the mail carrier, and the magicians. You may wish to have children begin their pantomime or play at the point in the tale where Mrs. Schmidt receives the package.

DISCUSSION OR WRITING PROMPT

Say: Mrs. Schmidt is too nosy. What's bad about being nosy? Can you think of any time when it might be good to be nosy?

Mrs. Schmidt and the Mysterious Delivery

A Romanian folktale as told by Jennifer Kroll

It was a little town. Everyone knew everyone. Everyone knew everyone else's business. And nobody knew more of everyone else's business than Mrs. Schmidt. Mrs. Schmidt had grown up and grown old in the little town. She lived in a little house that was crammed in tight next to many other little houses. That worked out well for Mrs. Schmidt. She could keep an eye on what was happening at the homes of many of her neighbors. She watched with interest when Mrs. Paulsen slipped on the ice and broke her hip. She tsk-tsked when Mr. Nelson sneaked out to have a cigar in the backyard. And she happily listened in on every spat of the young Fleishman couple. When a delivery truck came to a house, Mrs. Schmidt found out what was being delivered. If a plumber or doctor made a house call, she made sure she knew why. She quickly learned some juicy bit of gossip about anyone new to town. And she always made sure she spread the word.

One day, a "Sold" sign appeared in front of the vacant house down the street from Mrs. Schmidt's house. At once, Mrs. Schmidt started to nose about and find out what she could about the people moving in. What she heard was very interesting. Someone told her that the new people wore strange clothes because they were gypsies. Someone else claimed the new neighbors had been circus people. Mrs. Schmidt decided at once that these people would not make good neighbors. On and on she talked and complained about the new people she had not even yet met. "This town sure is going downhill," she'd say with a shake of her head. "I remember a time when only nice families lived on our end of town."

It couldn't have been much fun for the new people when they finally did move in. After all, Mrs. Schmidt had done her best to turn the neighborhood against them. But, as it turned out, Mrs. Schmidt had picked the wrong family to mess with. These new people were not gypsies. They weren't circus people, either. The husband and wife were, however, very powerful magicians.

It did not take them long to learn all about nosy Mrs. Schmidt and her gossiping ways. And they decided to teach her a lesson.

One day not long afterward, nosy Mrs. Schmidt looked out her window. She saw a mail carrier heading up the sidewalk toward her house. It wasn't her usual mail carrier, so of course that made her curious. And the box he was holding was simply huge! It was stamped all over with colorful stamps that said things like FRAGILE. She scurried to the door and opened it.

"Good day, ma'am," said the new mail carrier, "I'm so glad you're home. I have a package here for Mr. Paulsen next door. I wonder if you'd be kind enough to keep it on your porch until he gets back."

"Yes, of course," said Mrs. Schmidt. "I'd be happy to."

"Thank you, ma'am," the mail carried said. He gave her the package and left.

And so there stood Mrs. Schmidt, alone on her porch, holding the huge box. She turned it around and around, reading the stamps and stickers on it. CAUTION, one said. OPEN CAREFULLY, said another. ONLY TO BE OPENED BY ADDRESSEE, said a big sticker. Mrs. Schmidt could see that the box had been mailed from a distant country.

"What could possibly be in this box?" she muttered to herself.

She shook the box gently. She thought she could hear a strange humming sound coming from inside. The box seemed to smell a little strange, too.

"What could that Paulsen be getting up to these days?" Mrs. Schmidt wondered.

For all its stamps and stickers, the box didn't seem to be sealed very well. Across the top was a piece of packing tape. But the tape seemed mostly to have come unstuck. In fact, only the piece of twine around the box seemed to be holding it closed. And that twine was just looped once in each direction and knotted in one place.

Mrs. Schmidt set the box down in a corner of her porch. She went back inside to sweep her kitchen. But she couldn't stop thinking of the box. She kept going to the window to look at it. What was inside? It wouldn't take much to find out.

Mrs. Schmidt got her letter opener and went back out onto the porch. She glanced down the street in both directions. She was alone. She bent over the box and began to pick at the knot in the string. Mrs. Schmidt intended to take just a little look inside. Then she would tie the box shut again. The Paulsens would never even know what she'd done. And perhaps she would have some juicy bit of gossip to pass around. After a bit of work, the knot came loose. Mrs. Schmidt tugged the twine away, lifted the flap of the box and . . .

. . . screamed! Insects flew out of the box into her eyes and hair and onto her clothes. Grasshoppers jumped out and leaped across her porch. Termites and ants poured out of the box and swarmed up her porch railing.

"Oh no!" Mrs. Schmidt cried in dismay. "They're getting away!" She lunged toward some ants, scooped them up, and dumped them back into the box. "Get back in!" she cried. She grabbed a beetle out of her hair and flung it back in the box, too. "Stay there!" she screamed. But the insects poured out of the box faster than she could nab them and return them to it. "The Paulsens will find out what I've done! And tampering with mail is a crime!" Mrs. Schmidt remembered. She was in quite a panic.

Just then, a man and woman in colorful capes came walking past Mrs. Schmidt's porch. She recognized them as the new neighbors. "Good day," the man said to Mrs. Schmidt. "You look like you're having some trouble. What's the matter?"

"I can't catch them all!" Mrs. Schmidt cried, lunging here and there. "They're too small! They're too fast!"

"You mean those insects," the woman said. "Would you like me to help you catch them?"

"Yes! Yes!" cried Mrs. Schmidt. "Do anything you can!"

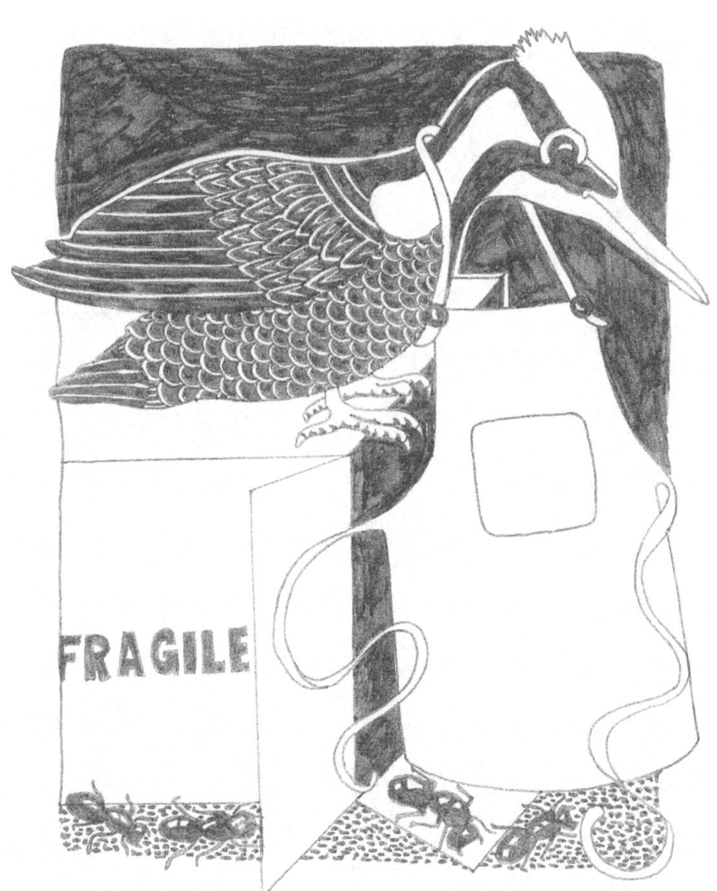

"All right then." And the woman drew a magic wand from her cape. "Here you are," she said. And with a zip and a zap, she changed Mrs. Schmidt into a woodpecker.

"Now you're all set, Mrs. Woodpecker," laughed the man in the cape. "Take that nosy nose of yours and catch all those bugs."

"Yes," said the female magician, returning her wand to her pocket. "For until you catch them all, my spell will hold."

And arm in arm, the two magicians walked off back to their house.

The woodpecker who had been Mrs. Schmidt was left to her job. And some people say that she's out there still, trying to find the last of those bugs. She's been looking for years now, in every tree trunk and branch in town. In fact, do you hear a tap-tap-tap coming from that tree over there? That just might be her. For until Mrs. Schmidt catches the last of those insects, the spell will not be broken.

 Mrs. Schmidt and the Mysterious Delivery

WOODPECKERS

- Bugs for breakfast? You bet! Woodpeckers like to eat many kinds of bugs, such as ants, beetles, and caterpillars. Their straight, strong beaks chisel into wood. They grab hidden bugs with their long tongues. Woodpeckers also eat plant foods such as seeds and berries. Some kinds of woodpeckers drink sap.

- What's home sweet home to a woodpecker? A nice cozy hole in a tree, usually. Woodpeckers use their beaks to dig out their nesting holes. Males and females work together. They line their nests with wood chips.

- Woodpeckers have four toes. Two of these toes face backward. The other two face forward. Their toes help them hang on.

- Woodpeckers have two strong tail feathers in the middle of their tails. They push the feathers against a tree branch or trunk. The special feathers help them to "walk" up a tree trunk without falling off.

- Some kinds of North American woodpeckers have red heads. Others just have a spot of red on their heads. Many females have no red on them at all.

- Tap-tap-tap-tap! Many people think this sound means a woodpecker is digging up her lunch. But woodpeckers can find their food without making much noise. They use their tapping sounds to send messages to other woodpeckers.

Be a Backyard Birder

Some kinds of woodpeckers like to visit bird feeders. One very common kind is the downy woodpecker. These birds are the size of a sparrow. Their wings have a black and white checkerboard look. To bring downy woodpeckers to your bird feeder, put out sunflower seeds or peanuts.

EXTENSION ACTIVITY: CODE WOODPECKER

Concepts: animal behavior/communication, developing a code, and deciphering coded messages

For this activity, you will need:

samples of woodpecker tapping sounds (available online—optional)

pencils

paper

rhythm instruments such as a woodblocks or sticks

- Read the **Feathered Facts File** with children. Discuss the fact that woodpeckers use their tapping sounds for communication. Have children guess at some of the things woodpeckers might want to say to each other. Share the fact that a woodpecker uses tapping to say, "This tree or area is mine," and also to invite a mate/friend to visit.
- Optionally, play samples of woodpeckers making tapping sounds or have children visit a Web site with samples of these sounds and listen on their own. Recordings of bird sounds—including woodpecker sounds—are available at allaboutbirds.com.
- Invite children to use rhythm instruments to imitate the tapping noises the woodpeckers are making.
- Pass out pencils and paper and have children write out the tapping patterns they are hearing/making.
- To extend the activity, invite pairs or groups of children to invent their own tapping languages. Have children develop tap combinations and write these down. Have them write the message each tap combination stands for. Messages might include "come here," "sit down," "stand up," "let's meet in the hall," "bring me an apple," or whatever children come up with.
- Have children memorize what the code sounds mean.
- Have the children test out their ability to send coded messages to each other by tapping with the rhythm instruments.
- To extend the activity even further, tell children about Morse code, or have them research in the library or online to find out more about this famous human method of sending messages by tapping.

Chapter 21

Wren

Appropriate for grades:

K-4

Reading level of story and fact file:

2.4

INTRODUCTION FOR PARENTS AND TEACHERS

The wren was an important player in the folk traditions of Ireland, Scotland, Wales, France, and the Isle of Man. In many communities, the strange custom of hunting for a wren was carried out on New Year's Day, the day of the winter solstice, or December 26 (a day known as Boxing Day or St. Stephen's Day). In some places, the body of a wren, or some substitute for it, is still paraded through the streets on that day (Tate 155–56). Participants in the parade may sing a song about how the wren is the king of all birds.

The featured story in this chapter explains how the tiny and seemingly lowly wren got to be the king of all birds. The tale was told throughout the British Isles and elsewhere. The Brothers Grimm included it in their *Kinder und Hausmarchen* in the early 1800s, and even an African version has been recorded. (See the Works Consulted list.) Features of the wren emphasized in the story include its small size and ability to remain hidden.

Although many different types of wrens can be found throughout the world, the most common and visible type throughout the Americas is the House Wren. The facts presented in the Feathered Facts File pertain to this common type of wren. Much of the information about wrens in this chapter, including that presented in the **Feathered Facts File,** is taken from Cornell University's *All About Birds* Web site. You can visit this site at http://www.allaboutbirds.org/guide/House_Wren/ to learn more about wrens, see photographs of these birds, and play recordings of their songs and calls.

A rhyming picture book that may inspire children to want to build birdhouses is Shirley Neitzel's *The House I'll Build for the Wrens*.

STORY SHARING STRATEGY

Pause after reading the opening paragraph of the story. Ask the children which type of bird they think will be selected as the leader of the birds. Have the children explain the reasons for their choices. Then read on to determine if any of the children have guessed correctly.

DISCUSSION OR WRITING PROMPT

Ask: Do you think the flying contest was a fair way of choosing who would be king? Why or why not? How do you think the birds should have picked their king?

The King of All Birds

Based on a folktale from the British Isles as told by Jennifer Kroll

One day, all the birds were talking together. They were trying to decide which bird they should choose as their leader. Many birds felt they should be chosen.

"I think I would make a great king," said Mockingbird. "I can speak many languages. And everyone stops to listen when they hear my lovely voice."

"You talk talk talk, that's for sure," laughed Cardinal. "But your feathers are so plain and gray. Red feathers like mine look much more kingly."

"A *few* bright feathers can be nice," agreed Mallard Duck. "But it's what you can do with your feathers that counts. And I am an expert at both swimming and flying."

And on and on they chirped and quacked and honked. Wise Old Owl listened quietly for a long time. And then she spoke up. "Whooo," she wondered. "Whooo can say which of us is greatest? We are all different and good at different things. That is the way we are made."

"But we *must* choose a leader," crowed Rooster, strutting through the crowd. He hoped the others would admire him and choose him for the job.

"Listen," said Eagle. "Wise Old Owl is right. We birds have many different talents. But there is one thing that we all can do. We can fly. So I say we have a flying contest to decide who gets to be the king or queen. Whoever flies the highest wins the throne."

Of course, it isn't true that all birds can fly. But most of the nonflying ones, such as penguins and peacocks, weren't there that day. So they really couldn't argue with Eagle. The birds in the crowd all quacked and cheeped and cawed and peeped and finally agreed to his plan. The Wise Old Owl would be the judge, they decided. The highest flier would become the new king or queen of the birds.

Now Eagle, of course, meant to win the contest. And when the others agreed to his plan, he smiled to himself. He thought he was as good as king already. For who can fly higher than an eagle?

"Ready? Set? Go!" cawed the Crow, and the many birds lifted off, all in one huge flock. They rose and rose and rose into the sky. After some time, a few fell behind and began drifting back toward the ground. Then more grew tired and gave up. Then more and more.

But Eagle was still climbing. Up and up. Soon, he was high above the others. He soared until he could climb no further. When he looked down, he saw no other bird anywhere near him. "I have flown the highest," he gasped. "I am the King of All Birds!" And he began coasting back to the ground.

But what Eagle didn't know was that a very small, clever bird had hidden itself in his wing feathers. This tiny bird named Wren had caught a ride up into the sky. Wren

was so small that Eagle had not even felt him there. But when Eagle cried out, "I am the King of All Birds," Wren popped out of his hiding place. "It's not true! I'm higher than you!" he sang out as he took off, zipping upward.

Eagle was furious. But he was also out of energy. "The little cheater!" he gasped, drifting toward the ground.

And that is how the tiny Wren became the King of All Birds. "It's not fair," sulked Eagle for years afterward. But he had to go along with the decision of the Wise Old Owl. And she said Wren was the winner.

"Whoooo can doubt Wren flew the highest?" Owl always said with a shrug. "Sometimes there's more than one way toooo get where you want to go."

 The King of All Birds

HOUSE WRENS

- House wrens are small brown birds with cream-colored tummies. A grown wren weighs only about the same amount as two U.S. quarters.

- Wrens might be small, but they have big voices! Many people like to hear wrens sing.

- House wrens live year 'round in South America. But in most U.S. states, you'll only see house wrens in the warmer months.

- Wrens look for a cozy little cave-like place where they can make their nests. They'll move into an opening in a tree trunk or wall. They've been known to build nests in empty cans and old boots. The male bird builds a few different nests at once. He lets his female friend decide which one she likes best.

- You won't see wrens at a bird feeder. Wrens don't eat seeds. They eat bugs such as flies, daddy longlegs, and caterpillars.

- Wrens weave spider egg sacs into the twigs and grass of their nests. That might sound weird. It makes sense, though. Wrens like to munch on spiders. And spiders might help the wrens in a different way, too. Spiders eat up small insects such as fleas and mites. These bugs may be living in the nest and bugging the birds.

Be a Backyard Birder

To bring wrens to your yard, buy or build a house with an opening that is 1⅛ inches. That's just the right size for wrens. And it's too small for most other birds.

EXTENSION ACTIVITY: BIG BIRD, LITTLE BIRD

Concepts: measurement, comparison, fractions (optional)

For this activity, you will need:

strips of paper

pencils

scissors

tape

a ruler

crayons or markers (optional)

- After the reading of the story, say: "You could probably tell from the story that a wren is much smaller than an eagle. We are going to compare the lengths of these two kinds of birds. Then you will be able to get a better idea of the difference in size."
- Next, have students use a ruler to measure out the lengths of the birds. Pass out strips of paper, pencils, and rulers to children. Say: "A wren is about 5 inches long." Have children mark paper strips at five inches and cut off the extra.
- Pass out a second paper strip. Say: "A bald eagle is about 30 inches long." Have children cut and tape paper strips together until they have a 30-inch-long strip. Have the children print *wren* and *eagle* on the two paper strips they have made. Children can also be prompted to draw a wren and an eagle on the two strips.
- Hold up the two strips of paper and say: "Let's see how much bigger the eagle is than the wren. How many times will our wren strip fit inside our eagle strip?" Prompt the children to place the wren strip at the edge of the eagle strip and make a pencil mark at the place where the wren ends. Children continue to mark off lengths of the wren until they reach the end of the eagle strip.
- Then, prompt the children to count up the number of wrens that fit inside the eagle strip. The answer will be six. Say: "So now we know that a bald eagle is six times longer than a wren."
- If appropriate, have children represent the difference as a fraction. Prompt them to tell you that a wren is 1/6 the length of an eagle.
- *Alternatively, with young children who are only doing nonstandard measurement,* give children a 5-inch strip of paper. Say: "This paper strip is about the length of a wren. An eagle is as long as about six wrens put together. Let's see how long that would be."
- Have the children measure out the length of six wrens on a piece of paper, a whiteboard, or a chalkboard.
- Have them draw and color an eagle of the length they've measured.

Works Cited

Annenberg Media. "Barn Swallow." *Journey North*. http://www.learner.org/jnorth/swallow/index.html.

Aristotle. *Nicomachean Ethics*. Trans. Martin Ostwald. New York: Macmillan, 1962.

Brown, Marcia, trans. *Cinderella or The Little Glass Slipper*. New York: Turtleback, 1997.

Burton, Robert. *The World of the Hummingbird*. Kingston, Ontario: Firefly Books, 2001.

Centers for Disease Control and Prevention. "Contributing Factors." *Overweight and Obesity*. http://www.cdc.gov/obesity/childhood/causes.html.

Cornell Lab of Ornithology. *All About Birds*. http://www.allaboutbirds.org/guide/search.aspx.

Fox and the Hound, The. Prod. Wolfgang Reitherman. Dir. Ted Berman and Richard Rich. Perf. Mickey Rooney, Kurt Russell, Pearl Bailey. Walt Disney Pictures, 1981.

Gonzales, Dafne. "Story Grammars and Oral Fluency." *The Journal of the Imagination in Language Learning* 5 (1999): 74–78.

Hayes, Joe. *Estrellita de Oro / Little Gold Star: A Cinderella Cuento*. El Paso, TX: Cinco Puntos Press, 2000.

Himmelman, John. *A Hummingbird's Life*. New York: Children's Press, 2000.

Hurston, Zora Neale. *Mules and Men*. New York: Harper Collins, 1935.

Ingersoll, Ernest. *Birds in Legend, Fable, and Folklore*. London: Longmans, Green, 1923.

Juster, F. Thomas, Hironi Omo, and Frank P. Stafford. *Changing Times of American Youth: 1981–2003*. Child Development Supplement. Anne Arbor: Institute for Social Research, University of Michigan, 2004.

Lee, F. H. "Why the Woodpecker Has a Long Beak." In *Folktales of All Nations*, 842. New York: Coward-McCann, 1930.

Linderman, Frank Bird. *Plenty Coups: Chief of the Crows*. Lincoln, Nebraska: University of Nebraska Press, 1957.

Louv, Richard. *Last Child in the Woods: Saving Our Children From Nature-Deficit Disorder*. Chapel Hill, NC: Algonquin Books of Chapel Hill, 2005.

McCloskey, Robert. *Make Way for Ducklings*. New York: Viking Press, 1941.

Milne, A. A. *The World of Pooh*. New York: Dutton, 1957.

National Academy of Sciences. *National Science Education Standards.* Washington, DC: National Academy Press, 1996.

National Council of Teachers of English. *NCTE/IRA Standards for the English Language Arts.* http://www.ncte.org/standards.

National Wildlife Federation. "What Is a Green Hour?" http://www.nwf.org/Get-Outside/Be-Out-There/Why-Be-Out-There/What-is-a-Green-Hour.aspx.

Neitzel, Shirley. *The House I'll Build for the Wrens.* New York: Greenwillow Books, 1997.

Pfeffer, Wendy. *Mallard Duck at Meadow View Pond.* Washington, DC: Smithsonian Backyard, 2001.

Pinkney, Jerry. *Aesop's Fables.* New York: SeaStar Books, 2000.

Politi, Leo. *Song of the Swallows.* New York: Aladdin Books, 1948.

Ring, Elizabeth. *Loon at Northwood Lake.* Norwalk, CT: Trudy, 1997.

Roberts, Donald F., Ulla G. Foehr, and Victoria Rideout. *Generation M: Media in the Lives of 8–18-Year-Olds.* Menlo Park, CA: Henry J. Kaiser Family Foundation, 2005.

Rockwell, Anne. *Two Blue Jays.* New York: Walker, 2003.

Ryder, Arthur W. *The Panchatantra: Translated from the Sanskrit.* Chicago: University of Chicago Press, 1925.

San Souci, Robert. *Little Gold Star: A Spanish American Cinderella Tale.* New York: HarperCollins, 2000.

Scheer, George F. *Cherokee Animal Tales.* Tulsa, OK: Council Oak Books, 1968.

Schulman, Janet. *Pale Male: Citizen Hawk of New York City.* New York: Knopf, 2008.

Scrace, Carolyn. *The Journey of a Swallow.* New York: Franklin Watts, 1999.

Tarbescu, Edith. *The Crow (Watts Library: Indians of the Americas Series).* New York: Scholastic, 2000.

Tate, Peter. *Flights of Fancy.* New York: Random House, 2007.

Wilde, Oscar. "The Happy Prince." In *The Complete Fairy Stories of Oscar Wilde* (pp. 7–19). Letchworth, UK: Duckworth, 1971.

Winter, Jeanette. *The Tale of Pale Male: A True Story.* New York: Harcourt, 2007.

Woods, Douglas. *Chickadee's Message.* Cambridge, MN: Adventure Publications, 2009.

Yolen, Jane. *Owl Moon.* New York: Penguin, 1987.

Works Consulted

CHAPTER 1: INTRODUCTION

Okie, Susan. *Fed Up! Winning the War against Childhood Obesity*. Washington, DC: Joseph Henry Press, 2005.

Tartamella, Lisa, Elain Herscher, and Chris Woolston. *Generation Extra Large: Rescuing Our Children from the Epidemic of Obesity*. New York: Basic Books, 2004.

CHAPTER 2: BLUE JAY

Claire, Elizabeth. *The Little Brown Jay: A Tale from India*. New York: Mondo Publishing, 1994.

Spellman, John. "The Beautiful Blue Jay." In *The Beautiful Blue Jay and Other Tales of India*. Boston: Little, Brown, 1967, 3–7.

CHAPTER 3: CARDINAL

"How the Redbird Became Red." *Canku Ota: An Online Newsletter Celebrating Native America*, no. 78, January 11, 2003. http://www.turtletrack.org/Issues03/Co01112003/CO_01112003_Redbird.htm.

Miller, Charlene. "How Red Bird Got His Color." Duvall, WA: Wilderness Awareness School, 2005–2008. http://www.natureskills.com/red_bird_story.html.

"Tell Me a Story: The Cardinal's Red Feathers (a Cherokee Tale)." *Times Herald-Record*, Record Online, July 27, 2009. http://www.recordonline.com/apps/pbcs.dll/article?AID=/20090727/LIFE/907270301/-1/LIFE.

Warren, Barbara Shining Woman. *How the Red Bird Got His Color*. Sugarland, TX: Powersource. http://www.powersource.com/cocinc/articles/redbird.htm.

CHAPTER 4: CHICKADEE

Bial, Raymond. *The Crow*. New York: Marshall Cavendish, 2006.

Gildart, Bert. "A Place of Peace." *Montana Outdoors* 35, no. 2 (2004): 16–21.

CHAPTER 5: CROW

Caxton, William. "Fable of the Crowe Whiche Was a Thurst." In *Caxton's Aesop*, ed. R. T. Lenaghan, 187. London: Oxford University Press, 1967.

The Crow and the Pitcher. Page by Page Books, 2004. http://www.pagebypagebooks.com/Aesop/ Aesops_Fables/The_Crow_and_the_Pitcher_p1.html.

Winter, Milo. "The Crow and the Pitcher." In *The Aesop for Children*, 34. New York: Barnes and Noble Books, 1993.

CHAPTER 6: DOVE

Cultural India. *The Hunter and the Doves.* http://www.culturalindia.net/indian-folktales/panchatantra-tales/unity-is-strength.html.

Panchatantra.org. *Second Strategy: Gaining Friends.* http://panchatantra.org/second-strategy-gaining-friends.html.

Pitara Kids Network. *The Wise Doves.* Kids Tailspin. http://www.pitara.com/talespin/folktales/online. asp?story=9.

Ryder, Arthur W. "The Winning of Friends." *The Panchatantra: Translated from the Sanskrit* 213–288. Chicago: University of Chicago Press, 1925.

CHAPTER 7: GULL

Kimmel, Eric. "Daedalus and Icarus." In *The McElderry Book of Greek Myths*, 68–75. New York: Margaret K. McElderry Books, 2008.

Morley, Jacqueline. "Daedalus and Icarus." In *Greek Myths*, 67–69. New York: Peter Bedrick Books, 1997.

Ovid. *Metamorphoses.* Book VIII: 152–235. Trans. A. S. Kline. Electronic Text Center, University of Virginia Library. Charlottesville: University of Virginia. http://etext.virginia.edu/latin/ovid/trans/ Metamorph8.htm#482327660.

CHAPTER 8: HAWK

Climo, Shirley. *The Persian Cinderella.* New York: HarperCollins, 1999.

Coburn, Jewell Reinhart. *Domitila: A Cinderella Tale from the Mexican Tradition.* Walnut Creek, CA: Shens Books, 2000.

Hickox, Rebecca. *The Golden Sandal: A Middle Eastern Cinderella Story.* New York: Holiday House, 1998.

Louie, Ai-Ling. *Yen-Shen: A Cinderella Story from China.* New York: Philomel Books, 1982.

Silverman, Erica. *Raisel's Riddle.* New York: Farrar, Straus, and Giroux, 1999.

CHAPTER 9: HUMMINGBIRD

Ortho Books staff. *How to Attract Hummingbirds & Butterflies.* San Ramon, CA: Ortho Books, 1991.

CHAPTER 10: LOON

Inuit Art Zone. "The Lumack Legend." From *Inuit Legends.* http://www.inuitartzone.com/en/about/about_ia_legends.html.

Maher, Ramona. *The Blind Boy and the Loon and Other Eskimo Myths.* New York: John Day Company, 1969.

Metayer, Maurice. "The Blind Boy and the Loon." In *Tales from the Igloo.* Edmonton: Hurtig, 1972.

Parker, Janet, and Julie Stanton, eds. "The Blind Boy and the Loon." In *Mythology: Myths, Legends, and Fantasies,* 471. Cape Town, South Africa: Struik, 2006.

CHAPTER 11: MALLARD DUCK

Arneach, Lloyd. "The Rabbit Goes Duck Hunting." In *Long Ago Stories of the Eastern Cherokee,* 79–85. Charleston, NC: History Press, 2008.

Duvall, Deborah L. *Rabbit Goes Duck Hunting.* Albuquerque: University of New Mexico Press, 2004.

Hanlon, Tina L. *The Rabbit, the Otter, and Duck Hunting.* At AppLit Home. http://www.ferrum.edu/applit/bibs/tales/duckhunting.htm.

Kirk, Lowell. "Cherokee Myths and Legends." Tellico, TN: Tellico Plains Mountain Press and *Tellico Times,* 1999. http://www.telliquah.com/cherokee.htm.

San Souci, Robert D. "Mistah Hare, Mistah Mink, and Miz Duck." In *Sister Tricksters: Rollicking Tales of Clever Females,* 36–41. Little Rock, AR: August House Press, 2006.

CHAPTER 12: MEADOWLARK

Curry, Jane Louise. "Bigfoot Bird." In *The Wonderful Sky Boat and Other Native American Tales from the Southeast,* 21–23. New York: Margaret K. McElderry Books, 2001.

Duncan, Barbara R. *The Origin of the Milky Way and Other Living Stories of the Cherokee.* Chapel Hill: University of North Carolina Press, 2008.

Encyclopaedia Britannica staff. *Treasure of American Wildlife: Prairie Animals.* Chicago: Encyclopaedia Britannica, 1979.

First People—The Legends. *Bigfoot Bird: A Cherokee Legend.* http://www.firstpeople.us/FP-Html-Legends/Bigfoot_Bird-Cherokee.html.

CHAPTER 13: MOCKINGBIRD

First People: The Legends. *How the Mockingbird Became the Best Singer.* http://www.firstpeople.us/FP-Html-Legends/How_The_Mockingbird_Became_The_Best_Singer-Mayan.html.

"How the Mockingbird Became the Best Singer." *Canku Ota: An Online Newsletter Celebrating Native America*, no. 105, January 24, 2004. http://www.turtletrack.org/Issues04/Co01242004/CO_01242004_Mockingbird.htm.

LaBastille, Anne. "How the King of Birds Was Chosen: And Other Mayan Folktales." *International Wildlife*, March–April 1997. http://findarticles.com/p/articles/mi_m1170/is_n2_v27/ai_19147416/?tag=content;col1.

CHAPTER 14: OWL

Giddings, Ruth Warner. "The Ku Bird." From *Yacqui Myths and Legends*. http://www.sacred-texts.com/nam/sw/yml/yml07.htm.

Hermann, Marjorie E. *El Pajaro Cu*. Lincolnwood, IL: National Textbook, 1996.

Vigil, Angel. "The Owl and the Painted Bird." In *From the Eagle on the Cactus*, 199–200. Englewood, CO: Libraries Unlimited, 2000.

CHAPTER 15: ROBIN

British Bird Lovers. *The Legend of Robin Redbreast*. http://www.britishbirdlovers.co.uk/articles/the-legend-of-robin-redbreast.html.

First People—the Legends. *Nukumi and Fire: A Micmac Legend*. http://www.firstpeople.us/FP-Html-Legends/Nukumi_And_Fire-Micmac.html.

Ketcham, Sallie. *The Christmas Bird*. Minneapolis, MN: Augsburg Fortress, 2000.

Merriam, C. Hart. *The Dawn of the World: Myths and Tales of the Miwok Indians of California*. Whitefish, MT, Canada: Kessinger, 2004.

Mosley, Cathy S. *How the Robin Got His Red Breast (Based on an Irish Folk Tale)*. East Lansing: Michigan State University, 1995–2007. Hnet. http://www.h-net.org/~nilas/seasons/robin.html.

The Sechelt Nation. *How the Robin Got Its Red Breast*. Gibsons, BC, Canada: Nightwood Editions, 1993.

CHAPTER 16: SPARROW

Livo, Norma J. "The Dance of the Monkey and Sparrow." In *Troubadour's Storybag: Musical Folktales from around the World*, 141–143. Golden, CO: Fulcrum, 1996.

Sakade, Florence, ed. "Monkey-Dance and Sparrow-Dance." In *Japanese Children's Favorite Stories*, 25–28. Boston: Tuttle Publishing, 2003.

CHAPTER 18: SWAN

Ganeri, Anita. "Siddhartha and the Swan." In *The Sound the Hare Heard and Other Stories*, 12–19. Laguna Hills, CA: QEB Publishing, 2007.

Mukherjee, Kanai L. "Buddha." At Indolink Kidz Korner: *Stories By Grandpa,* eds. Arundhati Khanwalkar and Bhibha Mukherjee. Association of Grandparents of Indian Immigrants. http://www.indolink.com/kidz/buddha.html.

"Prince Siddhartha's Kindness." *Life of the Buddha.* Buddha Dharma Education Association, 2008. http://www.buddhanet.net/e-learning/buddhism/lifebuddha/5lbud.htm.

"The Story of Buddha." *Between Sundays: Answering Kids' Questions.* Boston, MA: Church of the Larger Fellowship. http://clf.uua.org/betweensundays/middlechildhood/Buddha_story.html

CHAPTER 19: TURKEY VULTURE

Bascom, William Russell. "Waiting on the Lord." In *African Folktales in the New World,* 214–220. Bloomington, IN: U of Indiana Press, 1992.

Courlander, Harold. "Buh Buzzard and Salvation." In *A Treasury of Afro-American Folklore: The Oral Literature, Traditions, Recollections, Legends, Tales, Songs, Religious Beliefs, Customs, Sayings, and Humor of Peoples of African Descent in the Americas,* 474–475. New York: Basic Books, 1996.

Ruxton, Graeme D., and David C. Houston. "Could Tyrannosaurus Rex Have Been a Scavenger Rather than a Predator? An Energetics Approach." *Proceedings of the Royal Society of Biological Sciences* April 7, 2003, http://rspb.royalsocietypublishing.org/content/270/1516/731.full.pdf.

CHAPTER 20: WOODPECKER

Adams, Richard. "The Woodpecker." In *The Iron Wolf and Other Stories,* 43–46. London: Lane, 1980.

Retan, Walter. "Why the Woodpecker Has a Long Beak." In *Favorite Tales from Many Lands,* 40–43. New York: Grosset and Dunlap, 1983.

CHAPTER 21: WREN

"How the Wren Became King." From *Legends and Short Stories to Share on Bird Day.* Apples4theTeacher.com, 1999–2010. http://www.apples4theteacher.com/holidays/bird-day/short-stories/how-the-wren-became-king.html.

"Hunting the Wren on the Dingle Peninsula." *Ireland's Dingle Peninsula.* Kerry, Ireland: Dingle Peninsula Tourism, 1997–2009. http://www.dingle-peninsula.ie/wren.html.

King of the Birds: A Traditional Zulu Story. To be found on *CanTeach,* a Web site of elementary teacher resources. http://www.canteach.ca/elementary/africa7.html.

The Wren Song. On *Robokopp,* created and maintained by Richard Kopp, hosted by Musica International. http://www.musicanet.org/robokopp/scottish/thewren.htm.

Review of O'Faolain, Eileen, *The Wren, the King of the Birds.* On *Shvoong,* a Web site of reviews. http://www.shvoong.com/books/novel-novella/1723231-wren-king-birds/.

Ward, Helen. *The King of the Birds.* Brookfield, CT: Millbrook Press, 1997.

Zipes, Jack, trans. "The Wren." In *The Complete Fairy Tales of the Brothers Grimm,* 548–50. New York: Bantam Books, 1987.

Illustration Credits

All story illustrations are by Teresa DelVecchio. All rights reserved.

All coloring picture illustrations on Fact File pages were hand drawn by Jennifer Kroll, based on personal or public domain photographs. Thanks to the following photographers for use of their photographs as models.

Gary Kramer, U.S. Fish and Wildlife Service, mockingbird photograph

Ronald Laubenstein, U.S. Fish and Wildlife Service, great horned owl photograph

Steve Maslowski, U.S. Fish and Wildlife Service, loon photograph

Dave Menke, U.S. Fish and Wildlife Service, barn swallow, mourning dove, and woodpecker photographs

Falk Haehle, herring gull photograph

Gene Nieminen, U.S. Fish and Wildlife Service, swan photograph

Ken Thomas, blue jay photograph

Donna Dewhurst, U.S. Fish and Wildlife Service, chickadee and mallard photographs

Lee Karney, U.S. Fish and Wildlife Service, red-tailed hawk, robin, and hummingbird photographs

U.S. Fish and Wildlife Service (photographer not named), song sparrow photograph

John and Karen Hollingsworth, U.S. Fish and Wildlife Service, meadowlark photograph

Mike L. Baird, turkey vulture photograph

Index

About the Author

Jennifer L. Kroll, MAT, PhD, is former senior editor of Weekly Reader's *Read* magazine. Her published works include *Classic Readers Theatre for Young Adults* and Libraries Unlimited's *Weekly Reader's* Read *Magazine Presents Simply Shakespeare: Readers Theatre for Young People*. She lives in Connecticut with her husband, her two children, and a yard full of birds.